OVERLOAD

*Also by Linda Howard
from Severn House*

AGAINST THE RULES
ALL THAT GLITTERS
COME LIE WITH ME
THE CUTTING EDGE
DIAMOND BAY
HEARTBREAKER
AN INDEPENDENT WIFE
MIDNIGHT RAINBOW
SARAH'S CHILD
DUNCAN'S BRIDE
LOVING EVANGELINE
A GAME OF CHANCE

OVERLOAD

Linda Howard

This hardcover edition published 2020
in Great Britain and 2021 in the USA by
SEVERN HOUSE PUBLISHERS LTD of
Eardley House, 4 Uxbridge Street, London W8 7SY
by arrangement with Harlequin Books S.A.

British Library Cataloguing in Publication Data
A CIP catalogue record for this title is available from the British Library.

ISBN-13: 978-0-7278-9072-6 (cased)

All Severn House titles are printed on acid-free paper.

Severn House Publishers support the Forest Stewardship Council™
[FSC™], the leading international forest certification organisation.
All our titles that are printed on FSC certified paper carry the FSC logo.

Typeset by Palimpsest Book Production Ltd.,
Falkirk, Stirlingshire, Scotland.
Printed and bound in Great Britain by
TJ International, Padstow, Cornwall.

Chapter One

Thursday, July 21

It was hot, even for Dallas.

The scorching heat of the pavement seared through the thin leather of Elizabeth Major's shoes, forcing her to hurry even though it was an effort to move at all in the suffocating heat. The sleek office building where she worked didn't have its own underground parking garage, the builders having thought it unnecessary, since a parking deck was situated right across the street. Every time Elizabeth crossed the street in the rain, and every time she had risked being broiled by crossing it since this heat wave had begun, she swore that she would start looking for other office space. She always changed her mind as soon as she got inside, but it made her feel better to know she had the option of relocating.

Except for the parking situation, the building was perfect. It was only two years old, and managed to be both charming and convenient. The color scheme in the lobby was a soothing mixture of gray, dark mauve and white, striking the precise balance between masculine and feminine, so both genders felt comfortable. The lush greenery so carefully tended by a professional service added to the sense of freshness and spaciousness. The elevators were both numerous and fast and, so far, reliable. Her office having previously been in an older building where the elevator service had been cramped and erratic, Elizabeth doubly appreciated that last quality.

A private guard service handled the security, with a man stationed at a desk in the lobby for two shifts, from six in the morning until ten at night, as none of the businesses located in the building currently worked a third shift. Anyone wanting to come in earlier than six or stay later than ten had to let the guard service know. There was a rumor that the data processing firm on the tenth floor was considering going to three full shifts, and if that happened there would be a guard on duty around the clock. Until then, the building was locked down tight at 10:00 p.m. on weekdays and at 6:00 p.m. on weekends.

She pushed open the first set of doors and sighed with relief as the cool air rushed to greet her, washing over her hot face, evaporating the uncomfortable sweat that had formed in the time it had taken her to park her car and cross the street. When she entered the lobby itself through the second set of heavy glass doors, the full benefit of air conditioning swirled around her, making her shiver uncontrollably for just a second. Her panty hose had been clinging uncomfortably to her damp legs, and now the clammy feel made her grimace. For all that, however, she was jubilant as she crossed the lobby to the bank of elevators.

A big, unkempt man, a biker from the looks of him, entered the elevator just ahead of her. Immediately alert and wary, Elizabeth shifted her shoulder bag to her left shoulder, leaving her right hand unencumbered, as she stepped in and immediately turned to punch the button for the fifth floor, only to see a big, callused hand already pressing it. She aimed a vague smile, the kind people give each other in elevators, at the big man, then resolutely kept her gaze on the doors in front of her as they were whisked silently and rapidly to the fifth floor. But she relaxed somewhat, for if he was going to the fifth floor, he was undoubtedly involved, in some way, with Quinlan Securities.

She stepped out, and he was right on her heels as she marched down the hallway. Her offices were on the left, the chic interior revealed by the huge windows, and she saw that her secretary, Chickie, was back from lunch on time. Not only that, Chickie looked up and watched her coming down the hall. Or rather, she watched the man behind her. Elizabeth could see Chickie's big dark eyes fasten on the big man and widen with fascination.

Elizabeth opened her office door. The biker, without pausing, opened the door to Quinlan Securities, directly across the hall from her. Quinlan Securities didn't have any windows into the hallway, only a discreet sign on a solid-looking door. She had been glad, on more than one occasion, that there were no windows for more than one reason. The people who went through that door were ...*interesting,* to say the least.

"Wow," Chickie said, her gaze now fastened on the closed door across the hall. "Did you see that?"

"I saw it," Elizabeth said dryly.

Chickie's taste in men, regrettably, tended toward the unpolished variety. "He wore an earring," she said dreamily. "And did you see his hair?"

"Yes. It was long and uncombed."

"What a *mane!* I wonder why he's going into

Quinlan's." Chickie's eyes brightened. "Maybe he's a new staffer!"

Elizabeth shuddered at the thought, but it was possible. Unfortunately the "Securities" in Quinlan Securities didn't refer to the financial kind but the physical sort. Chickie, who didn't have a shy bone in her body, had investigated when they had first moved into the building and cheerfully reported that Quinlan handled security of all types, from security systems to bodyguards. To Elizabeth's way of thinking, that didn't explain the type of people they saw coming and going from the Quinlan offices. The clientele, or maybe it was the *staff,* had a decidedly rough edge. If they were the former, she couldn't imagine them having enough money to afford security services. If they were the latter, she likewise couldn't imagine a client feeling comfortable around body-guards who looked like mass murderers.

She had dated Tom Quinlan, the owner, for a while last winter, but he had been very close-mouthed about his business, and she had been wary about asking. In fact, everything about Tom had made her wary. He was a big, macho, take-charge type of man, effortlessly overwhelming in both personality and body. When she had realized how he was taking over her life, she had swiftly ended the relationship and since then gone out of

her way to avoid him. She would *not* lose control
of her life again, and Tom Quinlan had over-
stepped the bounds in a big way.

Chickie dragged her attention away from the
closed door across the hall and looked expectantly
at Elizabeth. "Well?"

Elizabeth couldn't hold back the grin that
slowly widened as her triumph glowed through.
"She loved it."

"She did? You *got* it?" Chickie shrieked,
jumping up and sending her chair spinning.

"I got it. We'll start next month." Her lunch
meeting had been with Sandra Eiland, posses-
sor of one of the oldest fortunes in Dallas.
Sandra had decided to renovate her lavish
hacienda-style house, and Elizabeth had just
landed the interior-design account. She had
owned her own firm for five years now, and this
was the biggest job she had gotten, as well as
being the most visible one. Sandra Eiland loved
parties and entertained often; Elizabeth couldn't
have paid for better advertising. This one
account lifted her onto a completely different
level of success.

Chickie's enthusiasm was immediate and
obvious; she danced around the reception area,
her long black hair flying. "Look out, Dallas, we
are cooking now!" she crowed. "Today the Eiland

account, tomorrow—tomorrow you'll do something else. We are going to be *busy.*"

"I hope," Elizabeth said as she passed through into her office.

"No hoping to it." Chickie followed, still dancing. "It's guaranteed. The phone will be ringing so much I'll have to have an assistant. Yeah, I like the idea of that. Someone else can answer the phone, and I'll chase around town finding the stuff you'll need for all the jobs that will be pouring in."

"If you're chasing around town, you won't be able to watch the comings and goings across the hall," Elizabeth pointed out in a casual tone, hiding her amusement.

Chickie stopped dancing and looked thoughtful. She considered Quinlan's to be her own secret treasure trove of interesting, potential men, far more productive than a singles' bar.

"So maybe I'll have *two* assistants," she finally said. "One to answer the phone, and one to chase around town while I stay here and keep things organized."

Elizabeth laughed aloud. Chickie was such an exuberant person that it was a joy to be around her. Their styles complemented each other, Elizabeth's dry, sometimes acerbic wit balanced by Chickie's unwavering good nature. Where Elizabeth was tall and slim, Chickie was short and voluptuous. Chickie tended toward the dramatic in clothing, so Elizabeth toned down her own choices. Clients didn't like to be overwhelmed or restrained. It was subtle, but the contrast between Elizabeth and Chickie in some way relaxed her clients, reassured them that they wouldn't be pressured into a style they weren't comfortable with. Of course, sometimes Elizabeth wasn't comfortable with her own style of dress, such as today, when the heat was so miserable and she would have been much happier in shorts and a cotton T-shirt, but she had mentally, and perhaps literally, girded her loins with panty hose. If it hadn't been for the invention of air conditioning, she never would have made it; just crossing the street in this incredible heat was a feat of endurance.

Chickie's bangle bracelets made a tinkling noise as she seated herself across from Elizabeth's desk. "What time are you leaving?"

"Leaving?" Sometimes Chickie's conversational jumps were a little hard to follow. "I just got back."

"Don't you ever listen to the radio? The heat is *hazardous*. The health department, or maybe it's the weather bureau, is warning everyone to stay inside during the hottest part of the day, drink plenty of water, stuff like that. Most businesses are opening only in the mornings, then letting their people go home early so they won't get caught in traffic. I checked around. Just about everyone in the building is closing up by two this afternoon."

Elizabeth looked at the Eiland folder she had just placed on her desk. She could barely wait to get started. "You can go home anytime you want," she said. "I had some ideas about the Eiland house that I want to work on while they're still fresh in my mind."

"I don't have any plans," Chickie said immediately. "I'll stay."

Elizabeth settled down to work and, as usual, soon became lost in the job. She loved interior design, loved the challenge of making a home both beautiful and functional, as well as suited to the owner's character. For Sandra Eiland, she wanted something that kept the flavor of the old Southwest, with an air of light and spaciousness, but also conveyed Sandra's sleek sophistication.

The ringing of the telephone finally disrupted her concentration, and she glanced at the clock, surprised to find that it was already after three o'clock. Chickie answered the call, listened for a moment, then said, "I'll find out. Hold on." She swiveled in her chair to look through the open door into Elizabeth's office. "It's the guard downstairs. He's a substitute, not our regular guard, and he's checking the offices, since he doesn't know anyone's routine. He says that almost everyone else has already gone, and he wants to know how late we'll be here."

"Why don't you go on home now," Elizabeth suggested. "There's no point in your staying later. And tell the guard I'll leave within the hour. I want to finish this sketch, but it won't take long."

"I'll stay with you," Chickie said yet again.

"No, there's no need. Just switch on the answering machine. I promise I won't be here much longer."

"Well, all right." Chickie relayed the message to the guard, then hung up and retrieved her purse from the bottom desk drawer. "I dread going out there," she said. "It might be worth it to wait until after sundown, when it cools down to the nineties."

"It's over five hours until sundown. This is July, remember."

"On the other hand, I could spend those five hours beguiling the cute guy who moved in across the hall last week."

"Sounds more productive."

"And more fun." Chickie flashed her quick grin. "He won't have a chance. See you tomorrow."

"Yes. Good luck." By the time Chickie sashayed out of the office, scarlet skirt swinging, Elizabeth had already become engrossed in the sketch taking shape beneath her talented fingers. She always did the best she could with any design, but she particularly wanted this one to be perfect, not just for the benefit to her career, but because that wonderful old house deserved it.

Her fingers finally cramped, and she stopped for a moment, noticing at the same time how tight her shoulders were, though they usually got that way only when she had been sitting hunched over a sketch pad for several hours. Absently she flexed them and was reaching for the pencil again when she realized what that tightness meant. She made a sound of annoyance when a glance at the clock said that it was 5:20, far later than she had meant to stay. Now she would have to deal with the traffic she had wanted to avoid, with this murderous heat wave making everyone ill-tempered and aggressive.

She stood and stretched, then got her bag and turned off the lights. The searing afternoon sun was blocked by the tall building next door, but there was still plenty of light coming through the tinted windows, and the office was far from dark. As she stepped out into the hall and turned to lock her door, Tom Quinlan exited his office and did the same. Elizabeth carefully didn't look at him, but she felt his gaze on her and automatically tensed. Quinlan had that effect on her, always had. It was one of the reasons she had stopped dating him, though not the biggie.

She had the uncomfortable feeling that he'd been

waiting for her, somehow, and she glanced around uneasily, but no one else was around. Usually the building was full of people at this hour, as the workday wound down, but she was acutely aware of the silence around them. Surely they weren't the only two people left! But common sense told her that they were, that everyone else had sensibly gone home early; she wouldn't have any buffer between herself and Quinlan.

He fell into step beside her as she strode down the hall to the elevators. "Don't I even rate a hello these days?"

"Hello," she said.

"You're working late. Everyone else left hours ago."

"You didn't."

"No." He changed the subject abruptly. "Have dinner with me." His tone made it more of an order than an invitation.

"No, thank you," she replied as they reached the elevators. She punched the Down button and silently prayed for the elevator to hurry. The sooner she was away from this man, the safer she would feel.

"Why not?"

"Because I don't want to."

A soft chime signaled the arrival of a car; the elevator doors slid open, and she stepped inside.

Quinlan followed, and the doors closed, sealing her inside with him. She reached out to punch the ground-floor button, but he caught her hand, moving so that his big body was between her and the control panel.

"You do want to, you're just afraid."

Elizabeth considered that statement, then squared her shoulders and looked up at his grim face. "You're right. I'm afraid. And I don't go out with men who scare me."

He didn't like that at all, even though he had brought up the subject. "Are you afraid I'll hurt you?" he demanded in a disbelieving tone.

"Of course not!" she scoffed, and his expression relaxed. She knew she hadn't quite told the truth, but that was her business, not his, a concept he had trouble grasping. Deftly she tugged her hand free. "It's just that you'd be a big complication, and I don't have time for that. I'm afraid you'd really mess up my schedule."

His eyes widened incredulously, then he exploded. "Hellfire, woman!" he roared, the sound deafening in the small enclosure. "You've been giving me the cold shoulder for over six months because you don't want me to interfere with your *schedule?*"

She lifted one shoulder in a shrug. "What can I say? We all have our priorities." Deftly she leaned past him and punched the button, and the elevator began sliding smoothly downward.

Three seconds later it lurched to a violent stop. Hurled off balance, Elizabeth crashed into Quinlan; his hard arms wrapped around her as they fell, and he twisted his muscular body to cushion the impact for her. Simultaneously the lights went off, plunging them into complete darkness.

Chapter Two

The red emergency lights blinked on almost immediately, bathing them in a dim, unearthly glow. She didn't, couldn't move, not just yet; she was paralyzed by a strange mixture of alarm and pleasure. She lay sprawled on top of Quinlan, her arms instinctively latched around his neck while his own arms cradled her to him. She could feel the heat of his body even through the layers of their clothing, and the musky man-scent of his skin called up potent memories of a night when there had been no clothing to shield her from his heat. Her flesh quickened, but her spirit rebelled, and she pushed subtly against him in an effort to free herself. For a second his arms tightened, forcing her closer, flattening her breasts against

the hard muscularity of his chest. The red half-
light darkened his blue eyes to black, but even so,
she could read the determination and desire
revealed in them.

The desire tempted her to relax, to sink bone-
lessly into his embrace, but the determination had
her pulling back. Almost immediately he released
her, though she sensed his reluctance, and rolled
to his feet with a lithe, powerful movement. He
caught her arms and lifted her with ridiculous
ease. "Are you all right? Any bruises?"

She smoothed down her skirt. "No, I'm fine. You?"

He grunted in reply, already opening the panel
that hid the emergency phone. He lifted the
receiver and punched the button that would alert
Maintenance. Elizabeth waited, but he didn't say
anything. His dark brows drew together, and
finally he slammed the receiver down. "No
answer. The maintenance crew must have gone
home early, like everyone else."

She looked at the telephone. There was no dial
on it, no buttons other than that one. It was con-
nected only to Maintenance, meaning they
couldn't call out on it.

Then she noticed something else, and her head
lifted. "The air has stopped." She lifted her hand
to check, but there was no cool air blowing from
the vents. The lack of noise had alerted her.

"The power must be off," he said, turning his attention to the door.

The still air in the small enclosure was already becoming stuffy. She didn't like the feeling, but she refused to let herself get panicky. "It probably won't be long before it comes back on."

"Normally I'd agree with you, if we weren't having a heat wave, but the odds are too strong that it's a system overload, and if that's the case, it can take hours to repair. We have to get out. These lights are battery operated and won't stay on long. Not only that, the heat will build up, and we don't have water or enough oxygen in here." Even as he spoke, he was attacking the elevator doors with his strong fingers, forcing them open inch by inch. Elizabeth added her strength to his, though she was aware that he could handle it perfectly well by himself. It was just that she couldn't tolerate the way he had of taking over and making her feel so useless.

They were stuck between floors, with about three feet of the outer doors visible at the bottom of the elevator car. She helped him force open those doors, too. Before she could say anything, he had lowered himself through the opening and swung lithely to the floor below.

He turned around and reached up for her. "Just slide out. I'll catch you."

She sniffed, though she was a little apprehensive

about what she was going to try. It had been a long time since she had done anything that athletic. "Thanks, but I don't need any help. I took gymnastics in college." She took a deep, preparatory breath, then swung out of the elevator every bit as gracefully as he had, even encumbered as she was with her shoulder bag and handicapped by her high heels. His dark brows arched, and he silently applauded. She bowed. One of the things that she had found most irresistible about Quinlan was the way she had been able to joke with him. Actually there was a lot about him that she'd found irresistible, so much so that she had ignored his forcefulness and penchant for control, at least until she had found that report in his apartment. She hadn't been able to ignore that.

"I'm impressed," he said.

Wryly she said, "So am I. It's been years."

"You were on the college gymnastics team, huh? You never told me that before."

"Nothing to tell, because I *wasn't* on the college team. I'm too tall to be really good. But I took classes, for conditioning and relaxation."

"From what I remember," he said lazily, "you're still in great shape."

Elizabeth wheeled away and began walking briskly to the stairs, turning her back on the intimacy of that remark. She could feel him right behind her, like a great beast stalking its prey. She pushed open the door and stopped in her tracks. "Uh-oh."

The stairwell was completely dark. It wasn't on an outside wall, but it would have been windowless in any case. The hallway was dim, with only one office on that floor having interior windows, but the stairwell was stygian. Stepping into it would be like stepping into a well, and she felt a sudden primal instinct against it.

"No problem," Quinlan said, so close that his breath stirred her hair and she could feel his chest brush against her back with each inhalation. "Unless you have claustrophobia?"

"No, but I might develop a case any minute now."

He chuckled. "It won't take that long to get down. We're on the third floor, so it's four short flights and out. I'll hold the door until you get your hand on the rail."

Since the only alternative was waiting there until the power came back on, Elizabeth shrugged, took a deep breath as if she were diving and stepped into the dark hole. Quinlan was so big that he blocked most of the light, but she grasped the rail and went down the first step. "Okay, stay right there until I'm with you," he said, and let the door close behind him as he stepped forward.

She had the immediate impression of being enclosed in a tomb, but in about one second he was beside her, his arm stretched behind her back with that hand holding the rail, while he held her other arm with his free hand. In the warm, airless darkness she felt utterly surrounded by his strength. "I'm not going to fall," she said, unable to keep the bite from her voice.

"You're sure as hell not," he replied calmly. He didn't release her.

"Quinlan—"

"Walk."

Because it was the fastest way to get out of his grasp, she walked. The complete darkness was disorienting at first, but she pictured the stairs in her mind, found the rhythm of their placement, and managed to go down at almost normal speed. Four short flights, as he had said. Two flights separated by a landing constituted one floor. At the end of the fourth flight he released her, stepped forward a few steps and found the door that opened onto the first floor. Gratefully Elizabeth hurried into the sunlit lobby. She knew it was all in her imagination, but she felt as if she could breathe easier with space around her.

Quinlan crossed rapidly to the guard's desk, which was unoccupied. Elizabeth frowned. The guard was always there—or rather, he had always been there before, because he certainly wasn't *now*.

When he reached the desk, Quinlan immediately began trying to open the drawers. They were all locked. He straightened and yelled, "Hello?" His deep voice echoed in the eerily silent lobby.

Elizabeth groaned as she realized what had happened. "The guard must have gone home early, too."

"He's supposed to stay until everyone is out."

"He was a substitute. When he called the office, Chickie told him that I would leave before four. If there were other stragglers, he must have assumed that I was among them. What about you?"

"Me?" Quinlan shrugged, his eyes hooded. "Same thing."

She didn't quite believe him, but she didn't pursue it. Instead she walked over to the inner set of doors that led to the outside and tugged at them. They didn't budge. Well, great. They were locked in. "There has to be some way out of here," she muttered.

"There isn't," he said flatly.

She stopped and stared at him. "What do you mean, 'there isn't'?"

"I mean the building is sealed. Security. Keeps looters out during a power outage. The glass is reinforced, shatterproof. Even if we called the guard service and they sent someone over, they couldn't unlock the doors until the electricity was restored. It's like the vault mechanisms in banks."

"Well, you're the security expert. Get us out. Override the system somehow."

"Can't be done."

"Of course it can. Or are you admitting there's something you can't do?"

He crossed his arms over his chest and smiled benignly. "I mean that I designed the security system in this building, and it can't be breached. At least, not until the power comes back on. Until then, I can't get into the system. No one can."

Elizabeth caught her breath on a surge of fury, more at his attitude than the circumstances. He just looked so damn *smug*.

"So we call 911," she said.

"Why?"

"What do you mean, why? We're stuck in this building!"

"Is either of us ill? Hurt? Are we in any danger? This isn't an emergency, it's an inconvenience, and believe me, they have their hands full with real emergencies right now. And they can't get into the building, either. The only possible way out is to climb to the roof and be lifted off by helicopter, but that's an awful lot of expense and trouble for someone who isn't in any danger. We have food and water in the building. The sensible thing is to stay right here."

Put that way, she grudgingly accepted that she had

no choice. "I know," she said with a sigh. "It's just that I feel so…trapped." In more ways than one.

"It'll be fun. We'll get to raid the snack machines—"

"They operate on electricity, too."

"I didn't say we'd use money," he replied, and winked at her. "Under the circumstances, no one will mind."

She would mind. She dreaded every minute of this, and it could last for *hours.* The last thing she wanted to do was spend any time alone with Quinlan, but it looked as if she had no choice. If only she could relax in his company, she wouldn't mind, but that was beyond her ability. She felt acutely uncomfortable with him, her tension compounded of several different things: uppermost was anger that he had dared to pry into her life the way he had; a fair amount of guilt, for she knew she owed him at least an explanation, and the truth was still both painful and embarrassing; a sort of wistfulness, because she had enjoyed so much about him; and desire—God, yes, a frustrated desire that had been feeding for months on the memory of that one night they had spent together.

"We don't have to worry about the air," he said, looking around at the two-story lobby. "It'll get considerably warmer in here, but the insulation and thermal-glazed windows will keep it from getting critically hot. We'll be okay."

She forced herself to stop fretting and think sensibly. There was no way out of this situation, so she might as well make the best of it, and that meant staying as comfortable as they could. In this case, comfortable meant cool. She began looking around; as he'd said, they had food and water, though they would have to scrounge for it, and there was enough furniture here in the lobby to furnish several living rooms, so they had plenty of cushions to fashion beds. Her mind skittered away from that last thought. Her gaze fell on the stairway doors, and the old saying "hot air rises" came to mind. "If we open the bottom stairway doors, that'll create a chimney effect to carry the heat upward," she said.

"Good idea. I'm going to go back up to my office to get a flashlight and raid the snack machine. Is there anything you want from your office while I'm up there?"

Mentally she ransacked her office, coming up with several items that might prove handy. "Quite a bit, actually. I'll go with you."

"No point in both of us climbing the stairs in the dark," he said casually. "Just tell me what you want."

That was just like him, she thought irritably, wanting to do everything himself and not involve her. "It makes more sense if we both go. You can pilfer your office for survival stuff, and I'll pilfer mine. I think I have a flashlight, too, but I'm not certain where it is."

"It's eight flights, climbing, this time, instead of going down," he warned her, looking down at her high heels.

In answer, she stepped out of her shoes and lifted her eyebrows expectantly. He gave her a thoughtful look, then gave in without more argument, gesturing her ahead of him. He relocated a large potted tree to hold the stairway door propped open, handling it as casually as if the big pot didn't weigh over a hundred pounds. Elizabeth had a good idea how heavy it was, however, for she loved potted plants and her condo was always full of greenery. She wondered how it would feel to have such strength, to possess Quinlan's basic self-confidence that he could handle any situation or difficulty. With him, it was even more than mere confidence; there was a certain arrogance, subtle but unmistakably there, the quiet arrogance of a man who knew his own strengths and skills. Though he had adroitly sidestepped giving out any personal information about his past, she sensed that some of those skills were deadly.

She entered the stairwell with less uneasiness this time, for there was enough light coming in through the open door to make the first two flights perfectly visible. Above that, however, they proceeded in thick, all-encompassing darkness. As he had before, Quinlan passed an arm behind her back to grip the rail, and his free hand held her elbow. His hand had always been there whenever they had gone up or down steps, she remembered. At first it had been pleasurable, but soon she had felt a little smothered, and then downright alarmed. Quinlan's possessiveness had made her uneasy, rather than secure. She knew too well how such an attitude could get out of hand.

Just to break the silence she quipped, "If either of us smoked, we'd have a cigarette lighter to light our path."

"If either of us smoked," he came back dryly, "we wouldn't have the breath to climb the stairs."

She chuckled, then saved her energy to concentrate on the steps. Climbing five floors wasn't beyond her capabilities, but it was still an effort. She was breathing hard by the time they reached the fifth floor, and the darkness was becoming unnerving. Quinlan stepped forward and opened the door, letting in a sweet spill of light.

They parted ways at their respective offices, Quinlan disappearing into his while Elizabeth unlocked hers. The late-afternoon light was still spilling brightly through the windows, reminding her that, in actuality, very little time had passed since the elevator had lurched to a halt. A disbelieving glance at her wristwatch said that it had been less than half an hour.

The flashlight was the most important item, and she searched the file cabinets until she found it. Praying that the batteries weren't dead, she thumbed the switch and was rewarded by a beam of light. She switched it off and placed it on Chickie's desk. She and Chickie made their own coffee, as it was both more convenient and better tasting than the vending machine kind, so she got their cups and put them on the desk next to the flashlight. Drinking from them would be easier than splashing water into their mouths with their hands, and she knew Chickie wouldn't mind if Quinlan used her cup. Quite the contrary.

Knowing that her secretary had an active sweet tooth, Elizabeth began rifling the desk drawers, smiling in appreciation when she found a six-pack of chocolate bars with only one missing, a new pack of fig bars, chewing gum, a honey bun and a huge blueberry muffin. Granted, it was junk food, but at least they wouldn't be hungry. Finally she got two of the soft pillows that decorated the chairs in her office, thinking that they would be more comfortable for sleeping than the upholstered cushions downstairs.

Quinlan opened the door, and she glanced at him. He had removed his suit jacket and was carrying a small black leather bag. He looked at her loot and laughed softly. "Were you a scout, by any chance?"

"I can't take the credit for most of it. Chickie's the one with a sweet tooth."

"Remind me to give her a big hug the next time I see her."

"She'd rather have you set her up on a date with that biker who came in after lunch."

He laughed again. "Feeling adventurous, is she?"

"Chickie's *always* adventurous. Was he a client?"

"No."

She sensed that that was all the information he was going to give out about the "biker." As always, Quinlan was extremely closemouthed about his business, both clients and staff. On their dates, he had always wanted to talk about *her,* showing interest in every little detail of her life, while at the same time gently stonewalling her tentative efforts to find out more about him. It hadn't been long before that focused interest, coupled with his refusal to talk about himself, had begun making her extremely uncomfortable. She could understand not wanting to talk about certain things; there was a certain period that she couldn't bring herself to talk about, either, but Quinlan's secretiveness had been so absolute that she didn't even know if he had any family. On the other hand, he had noticed the gap in her own life and had already started asking probing little questions when she had broken off the relationship.

There was a silk paisley shawl draped across a chair, and Elizabeth spread it across the desk to use as an upscale version of a hobo's pouch. As she began piling her collection in the middle of the shawl, Quinlan casually flicked at the fringe with one finger. "Do people actually buy shawls just because they look good draped across chairs?"

"Of course. Why not?"

"It's kind of silly, isn't it?"

"I guess it depends on your viewpoint. Do you think it's silly when people spend hundreds of dollars on mag wheels for their cars or trucks, just because they look good?"

"Cars and trucks are useful."

"So are chairs," she said dryly. She gathered the four corners of the shawl together and tied them in a knot. "Ready."

"While we're up here, we need to raid the snack machines, rather than rely on what you have there. There's no point in making extra trips upstairs to get more food when we can get it now."

She gave him a dubious look. "Do you think we'll be here so long that we'll need that much food?"

"Probably not, but I'd rather have too much than too little. We can always return what we don't eat."

"Logical," she admitted.

He turned to open the door for her, and Elizabeth stared in shock at the lethal black pistol tucked into his waistband at the small of his back. "Good God," she blurted. "What are you going to do with that?"

Chapter Three

He raised his eyebrows. "Whatever needs doing," he said mildly.

"Thank you so much for the reassurance! Are you expecting any kind of trouble? I thought you said the building was sealed."

"The building *is* sealed, and no, I'm not expecting any trouble. That doesn't mean I'm going to be caught unprepared if I'm wrong. Don't worry about it. I'm always armed, in one way or another. It's just that this is the first time you've noticed."

She stared at him. "You don't usually carry a pistol."

"Yes, I do. You wouldn't have noticed it now if I hadn't taken my coat off."

"You didn't have one the night we—" She cut off the rest of the sentence.

"Made love?" He finished it for her. His blue eyes were steady, watchful. "Not that night, no. I knew I was going to make love to you, and I didn't want to scare you in any way, so I locked the pistol in the glove compartment before I picked you up. But I had a knife in my boot. Just like I do now."

It was difficult to breathe. She fought to suck in a deep breath as she bypassed the issue of the pistol and latched on to the most shocking part of what he'd just said. "You *knew* we were going to make love?"

He gave her another of those thoughtful looks. "You don't want to talk about that right now. Let's get finished here and get settled in the lobby before dark so we can save the batteries in the flashlights."

It was another logical suggestion, except for the fact that night wouldn't arrive until about nine o'clock, giving them plenty of time. She leaned back against the desk and crossed her arms. "Why don't I want to talk about it now?"

"Just an assumption I made. You've spent over half a year avoiding me, so I didn't think you would suddenly want to start an in-depth discussion. If I'm wrong, by all means let's talk." A sudden dangerous glitter lit his eyes. "Was I too rough? Was five times too many? I don't think so, because I could feel your climaxes squeezing me," he said bluntly. "Not to mention the way you had your legs locked around me so tight I could barely move. And I know damn good and well I don't snore or talk in my sleep, so just what in hell happened to send you running?"

His voice was low and hard, and he had moved closer so that he loomed over her. She had never seen him lose control, but as she saw the rage in his eyes she knew that he was closer to doing so now than she had ever imagined. It shook her a little. Not because she was afraid of him—at least, not in that way—but because she hadn't imagined it would have mattered so much to him.

Then she squared her shoulders, determined not to let him take charge of the conversation and turn it back on her the way he had so many times. "What do you mean, you *knew* we would make love that night?" she demanded, getting back to the original subject.

"Just what I said."

"How could you have been so sure? *I* certainly hadn't planned on it happening."

"No. But I knew you wouldn't turn me down."

"You know a damn lot, don't you?" she snapped, incensed by that unshakable self-confidence of his.

"Yeah. But I don't know why you ran afterward. So why don't you tell me? Then we can get the problem straightened out and pick up where we left off."

She glared at him, not budging. He ran his hand through his dark hair, which he kept in a short, almost military cut. He was so controlled, it was one of the few gestures of irritation she could ever remember him making. "All right," he muttered. "I knew you were hiding things from me, maybe because you didn't trust what was between us. I thought that once we'd made love, once you knew you belonged to me, you'd trust me and stop holding back."

She forgot to glare. Her arms dropped to her sides, and she gaped at him. "I *belong* to you? I beg your pardon! Do you have a bill of sale that I don't know about?"

"Yes, belong!" he barked. "I had planned on marriage, kids, the whole bit, but you kept edging away from me. And I didn't know why. I still don't."

"Marriage? Kids?" She could barely speak, she was so astounded. The words came out in a squeak. "I don't suppose it ever occurred to you to let me in on all of this planning you were doing, did it? No, don't bother to answer. You made up your mind, and that was it, regardless of how *I* felt."

"I knew how you felt. You were in love with me.

You still are. That's why it doesn't make sense that you ran."

"Maybe not to you, but it's crystal clear to me." She looked away, her face burning. She hadn't realized her feelings had been so obvious to him, though she had known fairly early in their relationship that she loved him. The more uneasy she had become, however, the more she had tried to hide the intensity of her feelings.

"Then why don't you let me in on the secret? I'm tired of this. Whatever it is I did, I apologize for it. We've wasted enough time."

His arrogance was astonishing, even though she had recognized that part of his character from the beginning. Quinlan was generally a quiet man, but it was the quietness of someone who had nothing to prove, to himself or anyone else. He had decided to put an end to the situation, and that was that, at least from his viewpoint.

But not from hers.

"You listen to me, Tom Quinlan," she said furiously. "I don't care what plans you've made, you can just write me out of them. I don't want—"

"I can't do that," he interrupted.

"Why not?"

"Because of this."

She saw the glitter in his eyes and immediately bolted away from the desk, intent on escape. She was quick, but he was quicker. He seized her wrists and folded her arms behind her back, effectively wrapping her in his embrace at the same time. The pressure of his iron-muscled arms forced her against the hard planes of his body. Having seen him naked, she knew that his clothing disguised his true strength and muscularity, knew that she didn't have a prayer of escaping until he decided to release her. She declined to struggle, contenting herself with a furious glare.

"Cat eyes," he murmured. "The first time I saw you, I knew you were no lady. Your eyes give you away. And I was right, thank God. The night we spent together proved that you don't give a damn about what's proper or ladylike. You're wild and hot, and we wrecked my bed. You should have known there's no way in hell I'd let you go."

He was aroused. She could feel his hardness thrusting against her, his hips moving ever so slightly in a nestling motion, wordlessly trying to tempt her into opening her thighs to cradle him. It *was* tempting. Damn tempting. She couldn't deny wanting him, had never tried to, but he was right: she didn't trust him.

"It won't work," she said hoarsely.

"It already has." The words were soft, almost crooning, and his warm breath washed over her mouth a second before his lips were there, firm and hot, his head slanting to deepen the kiss and open her mouth to him. She hadn't meant to do so, but she found herself helpless to prevent it. Right from the beginning, his kisses had made her dizzy with delight. His self-confidence was manifested even in this; there was no hesitancy, no awkwardness. He simply took her mouth as if it were his right, his tongue probing deep, and a deep shudder of pleasure made her quake.

Held against him as she was, she could feel the tension in his body, feel his sex throbbing with arousal. He had never made any effort to disguise his response to her. Though it had been obvious even on their first date, he hadn't pressured her in any way. Maybe she had started falling in love with him then, because he had been both amused and matter-of-fact about his frequent arousal, his attitude being that it was a natural result of being in her company. She hadn't felt threatened in any way; in fact, looking back, she realized that Quinlan had gone out of his way to keep from alarming her. He had been remarkably unaggressive, sexually speaking, despite the persistent evidence of his attraction. She had never felt that she might have to face a wrestling match at the end of an evening. Even the night they had made love, she hadn't fully realized the seriousness of his kisses until she had somehow found herself naked in bed with him, her body on fire with need. Then she had discovered that he was very serious, indeed.

The memory made her panic, and she tore her mouth away from his. She had no doubt that if she didn't stop him now, within five minutes he would be making love to her. The hot sensuality of his kisses was deceptive, arousing her more and faster than she'd expected. It had been the same way that one night. He had just been kissing her; then, before she knew it, she had been wild for him. She hadn't known such intense heat and pleasure had existed, until then.

"What's wrong?" he murmured, reclaiming her mouth with a series of swift, light kisses that nevertheless burned. "Don't you like it? Or do you like it too much?"

His perceptiveness alarmed her even more, and despite herself she began to struggle. To her surprise, he released her immediately, though he didn't step back.

"Tell me what went wrong, babe." His tone was dark and gentle. "I can't make it right if I don't know what it is."

She put her hands on his chest to force him away and was instantly, achingly aware of his hard, warm flesh covered only by a thin layer of cotton. She could even feel the roughness of his hair, the strong, heavy beat of his heart pulsing beneath her fingers. "Quinlan—"

"Tell me," he cajoled, kissing her again.

Desperately she slipped sideways, away from him. Her body felt overheated and slightly achy. If she didn't tell him, he would persist in his seductive cajoling, and she didn't know how long she could resist him. "All right." She owed him that much. She didn't intend to change her mind about dating him, but at least he deserved an explanation. She should have told him before, but at the time all she had wanted was to stay as far away from him as possible. "But…later. Not right now. We need to get everything gathered up and get settled in the lobby."

He straightened, amusement in his eyes. "Where have I heard that before?"

"It isn't polite to gloat."

"Maybe not, but it's sure as hell satisfying."

She was nervous. Quinlan was surprised at the depth of her uneasiness, because that wasn't a trait he associated with Elizabeth. He wondered at the cause of it, just as he had wondered for the past six months why she had run from him so abruptly after spending the night in his arms. She wasn't afraid of him; that was one of the things he liked best about her. For him to find women attractive, they had to be intelligent, but unfortunately that intelligence tended to go hand in glove with a perceptiveness that made them shy away from him.

He couldn't do anything about his aura of dangerousness, because he couldn't lose the characteristics, the habits or the instincts that made him dangerous. He didn't even want to. It was as much a part of him as his bones, and went as deep. He had made do with shallow relationships for the sake of physical gratification, but inside he had been waiting and watching. Though the life he had led sometimes made him feel as if only a few people in this world really *saw* what went on around them, that most people went through life wearing blinders, now that he was mostly out of the action he wanted the normalcy that the average person took for granted. He wanted a wife and family, a secure, settled life; as soon as he had met Elizabeth, he had known that she was the one he wanted.

It wasn't just her looks, though God knew he broke out in a sweat at the sight of her. She was a little over average height, as slim as a reed, with sleek dark hair usually pulled back in a classic chignon. She had the fast lines of a thoroughbred, and until he had met her, he hadn't known how sexy that was. But it was her eyes that had gotten him. Cat eyes, he'd told her, and it was true, but though they were green, it was more the expression in them than the color that made them look so feline. Elizabeth's nature shone in her eyes. She had given him a warning look that had said she wasn't intimidated by him at all, underlaid by a cool disdain that was certainly catlike.

Excitement and arousal had raced through him. The more he'd learned about her, the more determined he had been to have her. She was sharply intelligent, witty, sarcastic at times and had a robust sense of humor that sometimes caught him off guard, though it always delighted him. And she burned with an inner intensity that drew him as inexorably as a magnet draws steel.

The intensity of his attraction had caught him off guard. He wanted to know everything there was to know about her, even her childhood memories, because that was a time in her life that would be forever closed to him. He wanted to have children with her and was fascinated by the possibility of a daughter in Elizabeth's image, a small, strongwilled, sharp-tongued, dimpled cherub. Talking about Elizabeth's own childhood made that possibility seem tantalizingly real.

At first Elizabeth had talked openly, with that faint arrogance of hers that said she had nothing to hide and he could like it or lump it. But then he had begun to sense that she *was* hiding something. It wasn't anything he could put his finger on; it was more of a withdrawal from him, as if she had built an inner wall and had no intention of letting him progress past that point.

Both his training and his nature made it impossible for him just to let it pass. Her withdrawal didn't make sense, because he *knew,* knew with every animal instinct in him that she felt the same way he did. She wanted him. She loved him. If she were truly hiding something, he wanted to know about it, and he had both the skill and the resources to find out just about anything in a person's life. His inquiries had turned up the fact that she had been married before, but the marriage had seemed to be fairly typical, and fairly brief, the sort of thing a lot of college graduates drifted into, quickly finding out they didn't suit. He'd had his own short fling with marriage at that age, so he knew how it happened. But the more he'd thought about it, the more he'd noticed that the period of her marriage was the one period she didn't talk about, not even mentioning that she'd ever been married at all. He was too good at what he did not to realize the significance of that, and he had begun to probe for answers about those two missing years. At the same time, feeling her slipping away from him, he had made a bold move to cement their relationship and taken her to bed, trusting in the bonds of the flesh to both break down the barriers and hold her to him until she learned to trust him completely.

It hadn't worked.

She had fled the next morning while he was still in the shower, and this was the first time he'd gotten her alone since then.

Over half a year wasted. Almost seven long damn months, endless nights spent in burning frustration, both physical and mental.

But he had her now, all alone, and before they left this building he intended to know just what the hell happened and have her back where she belonged, with him.

Chapter Four

"Let's get those snack machines raided," she muttered, grabbing up her ditty bag of goodies and heading for the door. Quinlan had been standing there, staring at her for what seemed like several minutes but had probably been less than thirty seconds. There was a hooded, predatory expression in his gleaming blue eyes, and she just couldn't stand there, like a tethered goat, for another second.

He sauntered out in her wake, and she relocked the office door, then looked up and down the dim hallway. "Just where *are* these snack machines?" she finally asked. "I'm not a junk food junkie, so I've never used them."

"There's a soft drink machine at this end of the hallway," he said, pointing, "but there are snack machines in the insurance offices. They have a break room for their employees, but they let us use them." He set off down the long hallway, away from the bank of elevators, and Elizabeth trailed after him.

"How are we going to get in?" she asked caustically. "Shoot the lock off?"

"If I have to," he replied, lazy good humor in his voice. "But I don't think it will come to that."

She hoped not. From what she could tell, insurance companies tended to be rather humorless about such things. She could well imagine receiving a bill for damages, which she could certainly do without.

Quinlan knelt in front of the insurance company's locked door and unzipped the leather bag, taking from it a small case resembling the one in which she kept her makeup brushes. He flipped it open, though, and the resemblance ended. Instead of plush brushes, there was an assortment of oddly shaped metal tools. He took two of them out, inserted the long, thin, bent one into the keyhole, then slid the other instrument in beside it and jiggled it with small, delicate movements.

Elizabeth sidled closer, bending down to get a better look. "Can you teach me how to do that?" she asked in an absent tone, fascinated with the process.

The corners of his mouth twitched as he continued to gingerly work at the lock. "Why? Have you just discovered a larcenous streak?"

"Do *you* have one?" she shot back. "It just seems like a handy skill to have, since you never know when you'll accidentally lock yourself out."

"And you're going to start carrying a set of locksmith's tools in your purse?"

"Why not?" She nudged the black leather bag with her toe. "Evidently you carry one in yours."

"That isn't a purse. Ah," he said with satisfaction, as he felt the lock open. He withdrew the slender tools, stored them in their proper places in the case and replaced the case in the bag. Then he calmly opened the door.

"Explain the difference between my purse and yours," she said as she entered the dim, silent insurance office.

"It isn't a purse. The difference is the things that are in them."

"I see. So if I emptied the contents of my purse into your leather bag, it would then become a purse?"

"I give up," he said mildly. "Okay, it's a purse. Only men don't call them purses. We call them satchels or just plain leather bags."

"A rose by any other name," she murmured with gentle triumph.

He chuckled. "That's one of the things I like best about you. You're such a gracious winner. You never hesitate at all to gloat."

"Some people just ask for it more than others."

She looked around, seeing nothing but empty desks and blank computer screens. "Where's the break room?"

"This way." He led her down a dark interior hallway and opened the last door on the right.

The room had two windows, so it wasn't dark. A variety of vending machines lined one wall, offering soft drinks, coffee, juice and snacks. A microwave oven sat on a counter, and a silent refrigerator stood at another wall. There was a vinyl sofa with splits in the cushions that allowed the stuffing to show, and a number of folding chairs shoved haphazardly around two cafeteria tables.

"Check the refrigerator while I open the machines," Quinlan said. "See if there's any ice. We don't need it now, but it would be nice to know that it's there just in case. Do it as fast as you can, to keep the cold air in."

"I do know about refrigerators and power failures," she said pointedly. Swiftly she opened the freezer compartment, and vapor poured out as cold air met warm. There were six ice trays there, all of them full. She shut the door just as fast as she had opened it. "We have ice."

"Good." He had the snack machine open and was removing packs of crackers.

Elizabeth opened the main refrigerator door but was disappointed with the contents. A brown

paper bag sat in lone splendor, with several trans-
lucent greasy spots decorating it. She had no
interest in investigating its contents. There was an
apple, though, and she took it. The shelves in the
door were lined with various condiments, nothing
that tempted her. The thought of putting ketchup
on the honey bun was revolting.

"Just an apple here," she said.

He finished loading his booty into the leather
bag. "Okay, we have cakes, crackers and candy
bars, plus the stuff you got from Chickie's desk. My
best guess is we'll get out of here sometime
tomorrow morning, so this should be more than
enough. Do you want a soft drink, or juice? There's
water downstairs, so we don't need to raid the drink
machines. It's strictly a matter of preference."

She thought about it, then shook her head.
"Water will be enough."

He zipped the bag. "That's it, then. Let's make
ourselves comfy downstairs."

"Should we leave a note?" she asked.

"No need. I'll take care of things when the power
comes on and everything gets back to normal."

The trip downstairs was considerably easier with
the aid of one of the flashlights, and soon they re-
entered the lobby, which was noticeably cooler
because of the two-story ceiling. She looked out
through the dark glass of the double entrance; the

street was oddly deserted, with only the occasional car passing by. A patrol car crawled past as she watched. "It looks weird," she murmured. "As if everyone has been evacuated."

"If the power doesn't come back on," Quinlan said in a grim tone, "it will probably get a lot busier once the sun goes down and things cool off a little. By the way, I tried to call out from my office, just to see what was going on and let someone know where we were, but I couldn't get a call to go through. If there's a city-wide blackout, which I suspect, the circuits will be jammed with calls. But I did find a battery-operated radio, so we'll be able to listen to the news."

"Turn it on now," she suggested, walking over to a sofa to dump her load on it. "Let's find out what's going on."

He opened the leather bag and took out a small radio, not even as big as her hand. After switching it on and getting only static, he began running through the frequencies, looking for a station. Abruptly a voice jumped out at them, astonishingly clear for such a small radio. "—the National Guard has been called out in several states to help prevent looting—"

"Damn," Quinlan muttered. "This sounds bad."

"Information is sketchy," the announcer continued, "but more reports are coming in, and it looks as if there has been a massive loss of electrical power across the Southeast and most of Texas."

"I'm not an expert," a second voice said, "but the southern tier of the country has been suffering under this heat wave for two weeks, and I imagine the demands for electricity overloaded the system. Have we had any word yet from the governor?"

"Nothing yet, but the phone lines are tied up. Please, people, don't use the telephones unless it's an emergency. Folks can't get through to 911 if you're on the phone to your friends telling them that your power's out, too. Believe me, they *know.*"

The second announcer chimed in, "Remember the safety precautions the Health Department has been telling us for two weeks. It's especially critical without electricity for air conditioning and fans. Stay out of the sun if possible. With the power off, open your windows for ventilation, and drink plenty of liquids. Don't move around any more than you have to. Conserve your energy."

"We'll be on the air all night long," said the first announcer, "operating on emergency power. If anything happens you'll hear it first here on—"

Quinlan switched off the radio. "Well, now we know what happened," he said calmly. "We'll save the batteries as much as we can."

She gave him a mock incredulous look. "What? You mean you don't have replacement batteries?"

"It isn't my radio."

It wasn't necessary for him to add that if it had been, of course he would have had extra batteries. She wished it *were* his radio. And while she was wishing, she wished she had left the building on time, though she wasn't certain she wouldn't be in a worse situation at her condo. Certainly she was safer here, inside a sealed building.

The magnitude of the problem was stunning. This wasn't something that was going to be corrected in a couple of hours. It was possible they would still be locked in at this time tomorrow.

She looked at Quinlan. "Are you *sure* it won't get dangerously hot in here?"

"Not absolutely positive, but reasonably sure. We'll be okay. We have water, and that's the most important thing. Actually, we're probably as comfortable as anyone in this city is, except for those places that have emergency generators. If we start getting too warm, we'll just take off some clothes."

Her heart literally jumped, sending her pulse rate soaring, and immediately she began to feel uncomfortably warm. Her stomach muscles clenched at the thought of lying naked in the darkness with him, but it was the tightness of desire. While her mind was wary, her body remembered the intense pleasure of his lovemaking. She turned back to the windows to keep him from reading her expression. Staring at the glass made her think of something else, and gratefully she seized on it.

"When it gets dark, will anyone on the outside be able to see us in here when we turn on a flashlight? Does the privacy glazing work at night?"

"Anyone who looked closely would be able to tell that there's a light in here, I suppose," he said thoughtfully. "But no one will be able to actually *see* us."

Just the possibility was enough. She had been about to arrange their supplies in the seating area closest to the entrance, but now she moved farther away. The lobby had several comfortable seating areas, and she chose one that was close to the middle. It was at least semiprivate, with a long, waist-high planter that created the sense of a small alcove. It was also closer to the bathrooms, making it a better choice all the way around.

She arranged their food supplies on a low table, while Quinlan shoved the chairs around to make more room. Then he collected cushions from the other chairs and stacked them close to hand, ready to make into beds when they decided to sleep. Elizabeth gave the cushions a sidelong glance. She wasn't sure she would be able to close her eyes with Quinlan so close by, or that it would be smart to sleep, even if she could.

She looked at him and started when she found him watching her. He didn't look away as he unknotted his tie and stripped it off, then unbuttoned his shirt down to his waist and rolled up his sleeves. His actions were practical, but the sight of his muscled, hairy chest and hard belly aroused a reaction in her that had nothing to do with common sense.

"Why don't you take off those panty hose?" he suggested in a low, silky voice. "They have to be damn hot."

They were. She hesitated, then decided wryly that it wasn't the thin nylon that would protect her from him. Only *she* could do that. Quinlan wasn't a rapist; if she said no, he wouldn't force himself on her. She had never been afraid of that; her only fear was that she wouldn't be able to say no. That was one reason why she had avoided him for the past six months. So leaving her panty hose on wouldn't keep him from making love to her if she couldn't say no, and taking them off wouldn't put her at risk if she did keep herself under control. It was, simply, a matter of comfort.

She got a flashlight and carried it into the public rest room, where she propped it on one of the basins. The small room felt stuffy and airless, so she hurriedly removed her panty hose and immediately felt much cooler. She turned on the cold water and held her wrists under the stream, using the time-proven method of cooling down, then dampened one of the paper towels and blotted her face. There. That was much better.

A few deep breaths, a silent pep talk and she felt ready to hold Tom Quinlan at arm's length for the duration. With her panty hose in one hand and the flashlight in the other, she returned to the lobby.

He was waiting for her, sprawled negligently in one of the chairs, but those blue eyes watched her as intently as a tiger watches its chosen prey. "Now," he said, "let's have our little talk."

Chapter Five

Her heart lurched in her chest. It strained her composure to walk over to the chairs and sit down, but she did it, even crossed her legs and leaned back as negligently as he. "All right," she said calmly.

He gave her that considering look again, as if he were trying to decide how to handle her. Mentally she bristled at the idea of being "handled," but she forced down her irritation. She knew how relentless Quinlan could be when crossed; she would need to keep her thoughts ordered, not let him trip her up with anger.

He remained silent, watching her, and she knew what he wanted. He had already asked the question; he was simply waiting for the answer.

Despite herself, Elizabeth felt a spurt of anger,

even after all these months. She faced him and went straight to the heart of the matter. "I found the file you had on me," she said, every word clipped short. "You had me investigated."

"Ah." He steepled his fingers and studied her over them. "So that's it." He paused a few seconds, then said mildly, "Of course I did."

"There's no 'of course' to it. You invaded my privacy—"

"As you invaded mine," he interrupted smoothly. "That file wasn't lying out in the open."

"No, it wasn't. I looked in your desk," she admitted without hesitation.

"Why?"

"I felt uneasy about you. I was looking for some answers."

"So why didn't you ask *me?*" The words were as sharp as a stiletto.

She gave him a wry, humorless smile. "I did. Many times. You're a master at evasion, though. I've been to bed with you, but I don't know much more about you right now than I did the day we met."

He neatly sidestepped the charge by asking, "What made you feel uneasy? I never threatened you, never pushed you. You know I own and run my company, that I'm solvent and not on the run."

"You just did it again," she pointed out. "Your ability to evade is very good. It took me a while to catch on, but then I noticed that you didn't answer my questions. You always responded, so it wasn't obvious, but you'd just ask your own question and ignore mine."

He surveyed her silently for a moment before saying, "I'm not interested in talking about myself. I already know all the details."

"I'd say that the same holds true for me, wouldn't you?" she asked sweetly. "I wanted to know about *you,* and got nowhere. But I didn't have you investigated."

"I wouldn't have minded if you had." Not that she would have been able to find out much, he thought. Great chunks of his life after high school graduation weren't to be found in public records.

"Bully for you. *I* minded."

"And that's it? You walked out on me and broke off our relationship because you were angry that I had you investigated? Why didn't you just yell at me? Throw things at me? For God's sake, Elizabeth, don't you think you took it a little far?"

His tone was both angry and incredulous, making it plain that he considered her reaction to be nothing short of hysteric, far out of proportion to the cause.

She froze inside, momentarily paralyzed by the familiar ploy of being made to feel that she was in the wrong, that no matter what happened it was her fault for not being good enough. But then she fought the memories back; she would never let anyone make her feel that way again. She had gotten herself back, and she knew her own worth. She knew she hadn't handled the matter well, but only in the way she had done it; the outcome itself had never been in question.

Her voice was cool when she replied. "No, I don't think I took it too far. I'd been feeling uneasy about you for quite a while. Finding that you had investigated me was the final factor, but certainly not all of it."

"Because I hadn't answered a few questions?" That incredulous note was still there.

"Among other things."

"Such as?"

In for a penny, in for a pound. "Such as your habit of taking over, of ignoring my objections or suggestions as if I hadn't even said anything."

"Objections to what?" Now the words were as sharp as a lash. His blue eyes were narrowed and vivid. A bit surprised, she realized that he was angry again.

She waved her hand in a vague gesture. "Any little thing. I didn't catalog them—"

"Surprises the hell out of me," he muttered.

"But you were constantly overriding me. If I told you I was going shopping, you insisted that I wait until you could go with me. If I wanted to wear a sweater when we were going out, you insisted that I wear a coat. Damn it, Quinlan, you even tried to make me change where I bank!"

His eyebrows rose. "The bank you use now is too far away. The one I suggested is much more convenient."

"For whom? If I'm perfectly happy with my bank, then it isn't inconvenient for me, is it?"

"So don't change your bank. What's the big deal?"

"The big deal," she said slowly, choosing her words, "is that you want to make all the decisions, handle everything yourself. You don't want a relationship, you want a dictatorship."

One moment he was lounging comfortably, long legs sprawled out in front of him; the next he was in front of her, bending over to plant his hands on the arms of her chair and trap her in place. Elizabeth stared up at him, blinking at the barely controlled rage in his face, but she refused to let herself shrink from him. Instead she lifted her chin and met him glare for glare.

"I don't believe it!" he half shouted. "You walked out on me because I wanted you to change banks? God in heaven." He shoved himself away from the chair and stalked several paces away, running his hand through his hair.

"No," she shouted back, "I walked out because

I refuse to let you take over my life!" She was unable to sit still, either, and surged out of the chair. Instantly Quinlan whirled with those lightning-quick reactions of his, catching her arms and hauling her close to him, so close that she could see the white flecks in the deep blue of his irises and smell the hot, male scent of his body. Her nostrils flared delicately as she instinctively drank in the primal signal, even though she stiffened against his touch.

"Why didn't you tell me you were married before?"

The question was soft, and not even unexpected, but still she flinched. Of course he knew; it had been in that damn investigative report.

"It isn't on my list of conversational topics," she snapped. "But neither is it a state secret. *If* our relationship had ever progressed far enough, I would have told you then. What was I supposed to do, trot out my past life the minute we met?"

Quinlan watched her attentively. As close as they were, he could see every flicker of expression on her face, and he had noticed the telltale flinch even though she had replied readily enough. Ah, so there *was* something there.

"Just how far did our relationship have to go?" he asked, still keeping his voice soft. "We weren't seeing anyone else. We didn't actually have sex until that last night together, but things got pretty hot between us several times before that."

"And I was having doubts about you even then," she replied just as softly.

"Maybe so, but that didn't stop you from wanting me, just like now." He bent his head and settled his mouth on hers, the pressure light and persuasive. She tried to pull away and found herself powerless against his strength, even though he was taking care not to hurt her. "Be still," he said against her lips.

Desperately she wrenched her head away. He forced it back, but instead of kissing her again, he paused with his mouth only a fraction of an inch above hers. "Why didn't you tell me about it?" he murmured, his warm breath caressing her lips and making them tingle. With his typical relentlessness, he had fastened on an idea and wouldn't let it go until he was satisfied with the answer. The old blind fear rose in her, black wings beating, and in panic she started to struggle. He subdued her without effort, wrapping her in a warm, solid embrace from which there was no escape.

"What happened?" he asked, brushing light kisses across her mouth between words. "What made you flinch when I mentioned it? Tell me about it now. I need to know. Did he run around on you?"

"No." She hadn't meant to answer him, but

somehow, caught in those steely arms and cradled against his enticing heat, the word slipped out in a whisper. She heard it and shuddered. "No!" she said more forcefully, fighting for control. "He didn't cheat." If only he had, if only his destructive attention had been diluted in that way, it wouldn't have been so bad. "Stop it, Quinlan. Let me go."

"Why did you start calling me Quinlan?" His voice remained low and soothing, and his warm mouth kept pressing against hers with quick, gentle touches. "You called me Tom before, and when we made love."

She had started calling him Quinlan in an effort to distance herself from him. She didn't want to think of him as Tom, because the name was forever linked in her mind with that night when she had clung to his naked shoulders, her body lifting feverishly to his forceful thrusts as she cried out his name over and over, in ecstasy, in need, in completion. Tom was the name of her lover; Quinlan was the man she had fled.

And Quinlan was the one she had to deal with now, the man who never gave up. He held her helpless in his grasp, taking kiss after kiss from her until she stopped trying to evade his mouth and opened her lips to him with a tiny, greedy sound. Instantly he took her with his tongue, and the sheer pleasure of it made them both shudder.

His warm hand closed over her breast, gently kneading. She groaned, the sound captured by his mouth, and desperately tried to marshal her resistance. He was seducing her just as effortlessly as he had the first time, but even though she realized what was happening she couldn't find the willpower to push him away. She loved him too much, savored his kisses too much, desired him too strongly, found too much pleasure in the stroke of those hard hands.

The pressure of his fingers had hardened her nipple into a tight nub that stabbed his palm even through the layers of fabric protecting her. He deepened the kiss as he roughly opened the buttons of her blouse and shoved a hand inside the opening, then under the lacy cup of her bra to find the bare flesh he craved. She whimpered as his fingers found her sensitive nipple and lightly pinched at it, sending sharp waves of sensation down to her tightening loins. The sound she made was soft, more of a vibration than an actual noise, but he was so attuned to her that he felt it as sharply as an electrical shock.

She was limp as he bent her back over his arm and freed her breast from the lace that confined it, cupping the warm mound and lifting it up to his hungry mouth. He bent over her, sucking fiercely at her tender flesh, wild with the taste and scent and feel of her. He stabbed at her nipple with his tongue, excited and triumphant at the way she arched responsively at every lash of sensation. She wanted him. He had told himself that there had been no mistaking her fiery response that night, but the six months since then had weakened his assurance. Now he knew he hadn't been wrong. He barely had to touch her and she trembled with excitement, already needing him, ready for him.

He left her breast for more deeply voracious kisses taken from her sweetly swollen lips. God, he wanted her! No other woman had ever made him feel as Elizabeth did, so completely attuned with and lost within her.

He wanted to make love to her, *now,* but there were still too many unanswered questions. If he didn't get things settled while he had her marooned here, unable to get away from him, it might be another six months before he could corner her again. No, by God, it wouldn't be; he couldn't stand it again.

Reluctantly he left her mouth, every instinct in him wanting to take this to completion, knowing that he could if only he didn't give her a chance to surface from the drugging physical delight, but he still wanted answers and couldn't wait, didn't dare wait, to get them. "Tell me," he cajoled as he trailed his mouth down the side of her neck, nibbling on the taut tendon and feeling the response ripple through her. Finally—*finally*—he was on the right track. "Tell me what *he* did that made you run from *me*."

Chapter Six

Frantically Elizabeth tried to jerk away, but he controlled her so easily that her efforts were laughable. Nevertheless, she lodged her hands against his heavy shoulders and pushed as hard as she could. "Let me go!"

"No." His refusal was flat and calm. "Stop fighting and answer me."

She couldn't do either one, and she began to panic, not because she feared Quinlan, but because she didn't want to talk about her marriage to Eric Landers, didn't want to think about it, didn't want to revive that hell even in memory. But Quinlan, damn his stubborn temperament, had fastened on the subject and wouldn't drop it until he got what he wanted. She knew him, knew that he intended to drag every detail out of her, and she simply couldn't face it.

Sheer survival instinct made her suddenly relax in his arms, sinking against him, clutching his shoulders instead of pushing against them. She felt his entire body tighten convulsively at her abrupt capitulation; her own muscles quivered with acute relief, as if she had been forcing them to an unnatural action. Her breath caught jerkily as her hips settled against his and she felt the thick ridge of his sex. His arousal was so familiar, and unbearably seductive. The lure of his sexuality pulled her even closer, her loins growing heavy and taut with desire.

He felt the change in her, saw it mirrored almost instantly in her face. One moment she had been struggling against him, and the next she was shivering in carnal excitement, her body tense as she moved against him in a subtle demand. He cursed, his voice thick, as he tried to fight his own response. It was a losing battle; he had wanted her too intensely, for too long. Talking would have to wait; for now, she had won. All he could think about was that she was finally in his arms again, every small movement signaling eager compliance. He didn't know what had changed her mind, and at this moment he didn't particularly care. It was enough that she was once again clinging to him, as she had the one night they had spent together, the night that was burned into his memory. He had tossed restlessly through a lot of dark, sleepless hours since then, remembering how it had been and aching for the same release, needing her beneath him, bewildered by and angry at her sudden coldness.

There was nothing cold about her now. He could feel her heat, feel her vibrating under his hands. Her hips moved in an ancient search, and a low moan hummed in her throat as she found what she had sought, her legs parting slightly to nestle his hard sex between them.

Fiercely he thrust his hand into her hair and pulled her head back. "Do you want this?" he asked hoarsely, hanging on to his control with grim concentration. It had happened so abruptly that he wanted to make sure before another second had passed, before she moved again and launched him past the point of no return. He hadn't felt like this since he'd been a teenager, the tide of desire rising like floodwaters in his veins, drowning thought. God, he didn't care what had caused her to change; right now, all he wanted was to thrust into her.

For a second she didn't answer, and his teeth were already clenching against a curse when she dug her nails into his shoulder and said, "Yes."

Her senses whirled dizzily as he lowered her to the floor, right where they stood. "The sofa..." she murmured, but then his weight came down on top of her and she didn't care anymore. Her initial tactic had been a panicked effort to distract him, but her own desire had blindsided her, welling up and overwhelming her senses so swiftly that she had no defense against it. She had hungered for him for so long, lying awake during the long, dark nights with silent tears seeping from beneath her lids because she missed him so much, almost as much as she feared him—and herself. The relief of being in his arms again was almost painful, and she pushed away all the reasons why this shouldn't happen. She would face the inevitable later; for now, all she wanted was Tom Quinlan.

He was rough, his own hunger too intense, too long denied, for him to control it. He shoved her skirt up to her waist and dragged her panties down, and Elizabeth willingly opened her thighs to receive him. He dealt just as swiftly with his pants, then brought his loins to hers. His penetration was hard and stabbing, and she cried out at the force of it. Her hips arched, accepting, taking him deeper. A guttural sound vibrated in his wide chest; then he caught the backs of her thighs, pulling her legs higher, and he began thrusting hard and fast.

She loved it. She reveled in it. She sobbed aloud at the strong release that pulsed through her almost immediately, the staggering physical response that she had known only with this man and had thought she would never experience again. She had been willing to give up this physical ecstasy in order to protect her inner self from his dominance, but oh, how she had longed for it, and bitterly wondered why the most dangerous traps had the sweetest bait.

Blinded by the ferocity of his own need, he anchored her writhing hips with his big hands and pounded into her. Dazedly she became aware of the hard floor beneath her, bruising her shoulders, but even as her senses were recovering from their sensual battering and allowing her to take stock of her surroundings, he gripped her even harder and convulsed. Instinctively she held him, cradling him with arms and legs, and the gentle clasp of her inner warmth. His harsh, strained cries subsided to low, rhythmic moans, then finally to fast and uneven breathing as he relaxed on top of her, his heavy weight pressing her to the floor.

The silence in the huge, dim lobby was broken only by the erratic intake and release of their breathing. His slowing heartbeat thudded heavily against her breasts, and their heated bodies melded together everywhere that bare flesh touched bare flesh. She felt the moisture of sweat, and the inner wetness that forcibly awakened her to the realization that their frantic mating had been done without any means of protection.

Her own heart lurched in panic; then logic reasserted itself and she calmed down. She had just finished her monthly cycle; it was highly unlikely that she could conceive. Perversely, no sooner had she had that reassuring thought than she was seized by a sense of loss, even of mourning, as if that panicked moment had been truth rather than very remote possibility.

"Elizabeth?"

She didn't open her eyes. She didn't want to face reality just yet, didn't want to have to let him go, and that was something reality would force her to do.

He lifted himself on his elbows, and she could feel the penetrating blue gaze on her face, but still she clung to the safety of her closed eyes.

She felt his muscles gathering, and briefly she tried to hold him, but he lifted himself away from her, and she caught her breath at the slow withdrawal that separated his body from hers. Despite herself, the friction set off a lingering thrill of sensation, and her hips lifted in a small, uncontrollable, telltale movement. Because there was no sanctuary any longer, she opened her eyes and silently met his gaze. That curious, sleepy blankness of sexual satisfaction was on his face, as she knew it must also be on hers, but in his eyes was a predatory watchfulness, as if he knew his prey had been caught but not vanquished.

His astuteness was disturbing, as it had always been. Her own gaze dared him to try to make anything more of what had just happened than an unadorned act of sex, without cause or future.

His mouth twisted wryly as he knelt away from her and pulled his pants up, zipping them with a faint, raspy sound. Then he got to his feet and effortlessly lifted her to hers. Her skirt, which had been bunched around her waist, dropped to the correct position. Elizabeth instinctively clenched her thighs to hold the wetness between them.

Quinlan shrugged out of his shirt and handed it to her, then leaned down and retrieved her panties from the floor. Thrusting them into her hands, too, he said, "Take off those clothes and put on my shirt. It's getting warmer in here, and you'll be more comfortable in something loose."

Silently she turned, picked up the flashlight and went into the ladies' rest room. Her knees were shaking slightly in reaction, and her loins throbbed from the violence of his possession. He hadn't hurt her, but it was as if she could still feel him inside.

She stared at her reflection in the mirror, the image ghostly with only the flashlight for illumination, making her eyes look huge and dark. Her hair had come loose and tumbled around her shoulders; she pushed it back distractedly, still staring at herself, then buried her face in her hands.

How could she go back out there? God, how could she have been so *stupid?* Alone with him for little more than an hour, and she had had sex with him on the floor like an uncontrolled animal. She couldn't even blame it on him; no, *she* had made the big move, grabbing at him, pushing her hips at him, because she had panicked when he had tried to pull back and begin asking questions again. She had gotten exactly what she had asked for.

She felt confused, both ashamed and elated. She was ashamed that she had used sex as an evasion tactic...or maybe she was ashamed that she had used it as an *excuse* to do what she had been longing to do anyway. The physical desire she felt for him was sharp and strong, so urgently demanding that stopping felt unnatural, all of her instincts pushing her toward him.

Her body felt warm and weak with satiation, faintly trembling in the aftermath. But now that he was no longer touching her, the old wariness was creeping back, pulling her in two directions. She had thought the decision simple, though it had never been easy, but now she was finding that nothing about it, either Quinlan or her own emotions, was simple.

Dazedly she stripped off her disheveled clothing

and used some wet paper towels to wash; the cool moisture was momentarily refreshing, but then the close heat of the rest room made sweat form almost as fast as she could wash it off. Ironically she admitted that, no matter how reluctant she was, she had no real choice but to face him again. If she remained in here, she would have heat stroke. It was a sad day when a woman couldn't even count on a rest room for sanctuary. Ah, well, she hadn't yet found any place that was truly safe from him, for her own memories worked against her.

Just as she pulled on her panties, the door was thrust open and Quinlan loomed in the opening, his big body blotting out most of the light from the lobby but allowing the welcome entrance of relatively cooler air. The subtle breeze washed around her body, making her nipples pucker slightly. Or was that an instinctive female reaction to the closeness of her mate? She didn't want to think of him in such primitive, possessive terms, but her body had different priorities.

He noticed, of course. His gaze became smoky with both desire and possessiveness as he openly admired her breasts. But he didn't move toward her, holding himself very still as if he sensed her confusion. "Hiding?" he asked mildly.

"Delaying," she admitted, her tone soft. She didn't try to shield her body from him; such an action would seem silly, after what they had just done. It wasn't as if he hadn't seen her completely naked before, as if they hadn't made love before. Moreover, he had decided to remove his pants and stood before her wearing only a pair of short, dark boxers. Barefoot and mostly naked, his dark hair tousled and wet with both sweat and the water he had splashed on his face, he was stripped of most of the trappings of civilization. Despite the heat, a shiver ran up her spine in yet another feminine response to the primitiveness of his masculinity, and she looked away to keep him from seeing it in her face.

He came to her and took up his shirt, holding it for her to slip into; then, when she had done so, he turned her and began buttoning the garment as if she were a child being dressed. "You can't stay in here," he said. "Too damn hot."

"I know. I was coming out."

He shepherded her toward the door, his hand on her back. She wondered if the action was just his usual take-charge attitude, or if he was acting on some primitive instinct of his own, to keep the female from bolting. Probably a mixture of the two, she thought, and sighed.

He had been busy while she had been in the rest room, and she realized she had delayed in there much longer than she had intended. He had arranged the extra cushions on the floor—in the shape of a double bed, she noticed—and gotten some cool water from the fountain, the cups ready for them to drink. The water was welcome, but if he thought she was going to docilely stretch out on those cushions, he would shortly be disillusioned. She sat down in a chair and reached for a cup, sipping it without enthusiasm at first, then more eagerly as she rediscovered how good plain water was for quenching thirst. It was a delight of childhood that tended to be forgotten in the adult world of coffee, tea and wine spritzers.

"Are you hungry?" he asked.

"No." How could she be hungry? Her nerves were so tightly drawn that she didn't think she would be able to eat until they got out of here.

"Well, I am." He tore open the wrapping on the big blueberry muffin and began eating. "Tell me about your marriage."

She stiffened and glared at him. "It wasn't a good marriage," she said tightly. "It also isn't any of your business."

He glanced pointedly at the floor where they had so recently made love. "That's debatable. Okay, let's try it this way. I'll tell you about my marriage if you'll tell me about yours. No evasion tactics. I'll answer any question you ask."

She stared at him in shock. "*Your* marriage?"

He shrugged. "Sure. Hell, I'm thirty-seven years old. I haven't lived my entire life in a vacuum."

"You have your nerve!" she flared. "You jumped down my throat for not talking about my past marriage when you've only now mentioned your own?"

He rubbed the side of his nose and gave her a faintly sheepish look. "That occurred to me," he admitted.

"Well, let me put another thought in your dim Neanderthal brain! The time for heart-to-heart confidences was over a long time ago. We aren't involved any longer, so there's no point in 'sharing.'"

He took another bite of the muffin. "Don't kid yourself. What we just did felt pretty damn involved to me."

"That was just sex," she said dismissively. "It had been a while, and I needed it."

"I know exactly how long it had been." His blue gaze sharpened, and she knew he hadn't liked her comment. "You haven't gone out with anyone else since you walked out on me."

She was enraged all over again. "Have you had me followed?"

He had, but he wasn't about to tell her that now. Instead he said, "Chickie worries because your social life, in her words, resembles Death Valley— nothing of interest moving around."

Elizabeth snorted, but she was mollified, because she had heard Chickie make that exact comment on a couple of occasions. Still, she would have to have a word with her about discretion.

"I've been busy," she said, not caring if he believed her or not, though it happened to be the truth. She had deliberately been as busy as she could manage in order to give herself less free time to think about him.

"I know. You've found a lot of lilies to gild."

Her teeth closed with a snap. "That's so people will have a reason to install your fancy security systems. I gild the lilies, and you protect them."

"I protect *people*," he clarified.

"Uh-huh. That's why you set up so many security systems for people who live in rough neighborhoods, where their lives are really in danger."

"I can see we aren't going to agree on this."

"You brought it up."

"My mistake. Let's get back to the original subject, namely our respective failed marriages. Go ahead, ask me anything you want."

The perfect response, of course, was that she wasn't interested. It would also be a lie, because she was not only interested, she was suddenly, violently jealous of that unknown, hitherto unsuspected woman who had been his wife, who had shared his name and his bed for a time, and who had been, in the eyes of the world, his mate. Elizabeth firmly kept her mouth closed, but she couldn't stop herself from glaring at him.

Quinlan sighed. "All right, I'll tell you the boring facts without making you ask. Her name was Amy. We dated during college. Then, when college was finished, it seemed like we should do adult things, so we got married. But I was away on my job a lot, and Amy found someone in the office where she worked who she liked a lot better. Within six months of getting married we knew it had been a mistake, but we held out for another year, trying to make it 'work,' before we both realized we were just wasting time. The divorce was a relief for both of us. End of story."

She was still glaring at him. "I don't even know where you went to college."

He sighed again. She was getting damn tired of that sigh, as if he were being so noble in his dealings with an irrational woman. "Cal Tech."

"Ah." Well, that explained his expertise with electronics and computers and things.

"No children," he added.

"I should hope not!" It was bad enough that he had, for some reason, concealed all the rest of the details of his life. "If you'd kept *children* hidden, I would never have forgiven you."

His eyes gleamed. "Does this mean you *have?*"

"No."

He gave a startled shout of laughter. "God, I've missed you. You don't dissemble at all. If you're grouchy, you don't feel any need at all to make nice and pretend to be sweetness and light, do you?"

She gave him a haughty look. "I'm not sweetness and light."

"Thank God," he said fervently. He leaned back and spread his hands, then stretched his long, muscular legs out before him in a posture of complete relaxation. "Okay, it's your turn. Tell me all the deep, dark secrets about *your* marriage."

Chapter Seven

"Show-and-tell was your idea, not mine." Her throat tightened at the idea of rehashing the details, reliving the nightmare even in thought. She just couldn't do it.

"You asked questions."

"I asked where you went to college, hardly the same as prying into your private life." Agitated, she stood up and longingly looked through the huge windows to the world outside. Only two thin sheets of transparent material kept her prisoner here with him, but it would take a car ramming into the glass at respectable speed to break it. The glass looked fragile but wasn't, whereas she was the opposite. She looked calm and capable, but inside she hid a weakness that terrified her.

"Don't run away," Quinlan warned softly.

She barely glanced at him as she edged out of the semicircle of sofa and chairs. "I'm not running," she denied, knowing that it wasn't the truth. "It's cooler moving around."

Silently Quinlan got to his feet and paced after her, big and virtually naked, the dark boxer shorts nothing more than the modern version of the loincloth. His muscled chest was hairy, the thick curls almost hiding his small nipples, and a silky line of hair ran down the center of his abdomen to his groin. His long legs were also covered with hair, finer and straighter, but he was undoubtedly a dominating male animal in his prime. Elizabeth gave him a distracted, vaguely alarmed look that suddenly focused on his loins, and her eyes widened.

He looked down at himself and shrugged, not pausing in his slow, relentless pursuit. "I know, at my age I shouldn't have recovered this fast. I usually don't," he said thoughtfully. "It's just my reaction to you. Come here, sweetheart." His voice had turned soft and cajoling.

Wildly Elizabeth wondered if this was going to degenerate into the stereotypical chase around the furniture. On the heels of that thought came the certain knowledge that if she ran, Quinlan would definitely chase her, instinctively, the marauding male subduing the reluctant female. She could prevent that farce by not running, thereby giving him nothing to chase. On the other hand, if she stood still things would only reach the same conclusion at a faster pace. Evidently the only real choice she had was whether or not to hold on to her dignity. If she had felt differently about him she could have said "no," but she had already faced that weakness in herself. For right now, in these circumstances, she couldn't resist him—and they both knew it.

He drew closer, his eyes gleaming. "For tonight, you're mine," he murmured. "Let me at least have that. You can't get away from me here. You don't even want to get away, not really. The circumstances aren't normal. When we get out of here you'll have options, but right now you're forced to be with me. Whatever happens won't be your fault. Just let go and forget about it."

She drew a deep, shuddering breath. "Pretty good psychologist, aren't you? But I'm not a coward. I'm responsible for whatever decisions I make, period."

He had reached her now, one arm sliding around her back. Elizabeth looked up at him, at the tousled dark hair and intense blue eyes, and her heart squeezed. "All right," she whispered. "For tonight. For as long as we're locked in here." She closed her eyes, shivering with sensual anticipation. She would let herself have this, just for now; she would feast on him, drown herself in sensation, let the darkness of the night wrap protectively around them and hold off thought. The time would come all too soon when she would have to push him away again; why waste even one precious minute by fighting both him and herself?

"Anything," she heard herself say as he lifted her. Her voice sounded strange to her, thick, drugged with desire. "For tonight."

His low, rough laugh wasn't quite steady as he lowered her to the cushions. "Anything?" he asked. "You could be letting yourself in for an interesting night."

She put out her hand and touched his bare chest. "Yes," she purred. "I could be."

"Cat." His breathing was fast and unsteady as he swiftly stripped her panties down her legs and tossed them to the side. "You won't be needing those again tonight."

She pulled at the waistband of his shorts. "And you won't be needing these."

"Hell, I only kept them on because I figured you'd fight like a wildcat if I came after you stark naked." He dealt with his shorts as rapidly as he had her underwear.

She was already excited by the anticipation of his slow, thorough loveplay. Quinlan was a man who enjoyed the preliminaries and prolonged them, as she had learned during the one night she had spent with him. It didn't happen this time, though. He pushed her legs open, knelt between them and entered her with a heavy thrust that jarred her. The shock of it reverberated through her body; then her inner muscles clamped down in an effort to slow that inexorable invasion.

He pushed deeper, groaning at the tightness of her, until he was in her to the hilt. She writhed, reaching down to grasp his thighs and hold him there, but he slowly withdrew, then just as slowly pushed back into her.

"Did your husband make you feel like this?" he whispered.

Her head rolled on the cushions at the speed and intensity of the sensations. It was an effort to concentrate on his words. "N-no," she finally sighed.

"Good." He couldn't keep the savage satisfaction out of his voice. He didn't like the thought of anyone else pleasing her. This was something she had known only with him; he had realized it immediately when they had first made love, but he had needed to hear her say it, admit that she had given her response to no one else.

He teased her with another slow withdrawal and thrust. "What did he do to you?" he murmured, and pulled completely away from her.

Her eyes opened in protest and she reached for him, moaning low in her throat as she tried to re-establish that delicious contact. Then comprehension made her eyes flare wider, and she jerked backward, away from him, trying to sit up. "You bastard!" she said in a strangled tone.

Quinlan caught her hips and dragged her back, slipping into her once again. "Tell me," he said relentlessly. "Did he mistreat you? Hurt you in any way? What in hell did he do that you're making me pay for?"

Elizabeth wrenched away from him again. She felt ill, all desire gone. How could he have done that to her? She fought to cover herself with his shirt, all the while calling herself several harsh names for her stupidity in thinking they could have this night, that she could give herself a block of time unattached to either past or present. She should have remembered that Quinlan never gave up.

No, he never gave up. So why didn't she tell him? It wouldn't be easy for her to relive it, but at least then he would know why she refused to allow him any authority in her life, why she had denied herself the love she so desperately wanted to give him.

She curled away from him, letting her head fall forward onto her knees so her hair hid her face. He tried to pull her back into his arms, into his lovemaking, but she resisted him, her body stiff in reaction to the memories already swamping her.

"Don't touch me!" she said hoarsely. "You wanted to know, so sit there and listen, but don't— don't touch me."

Quinlan frowned, feeling vaguely uneasy. He had deliberately pushed her, though he hadn't intended to push so hard that she withdrew from him, but that was what had happened. His body was still tight with desire, demanding release. He ground his teeth together, grimly reaching for control; if Elizabeth was ready to talk, after all these months, then he was damn well going to listen.

She didn't lift her head from her knees, but in the silent, darkening lobby, he could plainly hear every soft word.

"I met him when I was a senior in college. Eric. Eric Landers. But you already know his name, don't you? It was in your damn report. He owned an upscale decorating firm, and getting a part-time job there was a real plum."

She sighed. The little sound was sad, and a bit tired. "He was thirty-five. I was twenty-one. And he was handsome, sophisticated, self-assured, worldly, with quite a reputation as both a ladies' man and a well-known professional. I was more than flattered when he asked me out, I was absolutely giddy. Chickie would seem grim compared to the way I felt.

"We dated for about three months before he asked me to marry him, and for three months I felt like a princess. He took me everywhere, wined and dined me at the best places. He was interested in every minute of my day, in everything I did. A real princess couldn't have been more coddled. I was a virgin—a bit unusual, to stay that way through college, but I'd been studying hard and working part-time jobs, too, and I hadn't had time for much socializing. Eric didn't push me for sex. He said he could wait until our wedding night, that since I had remained a virgin that long, he wanted to give me all the traditional trappings."

"Let me guess," Quinlan said grimly. "He was gay."

She shook her head. "No. His ladies' man reputation was for real. Eric was very gentle with me on our wedding night. I'll give him that. He never mistreated me that way."

"If you don't mind," Quinlan interrupted, his teeth coming together with an audible snap, "I'd rather not hear about your sex life with him, if that wasn't the problem."

Elizabeth was surprised into lifting her head. "Are you jealous?" she asked warily.

He rubbed his hand over his jaw; as late in the day as it was, his five-o'clock shadow had become more substantial and made a rasping sound as his hand

passed over it. "Not jealous, exactly," he muttered.
"I just don't want to hear it, if you enjoyed making
love with him. Hell, *yes,* I'm jealous!"

She gave a spurt of laughter, startling herself.
She had never expected to be able to laugh while
discussing Eric Landers, but Quinlan's frustration
was so obvious that she couldn't help it.

"I don't mind giving the devil his due," she said in
a generous tone. "You can pat yourself on the back,
because you know you were the first to—umm—"

"Satisfy you," he supplied. A sheepish expression crossed his face.

"I'm not very experienced. You're the only man
I've gone to bed with since my divorce. After Eric,
I just didn't want to let anyone close to me."

She didn't continue, and the silence stretched
between them. It was growing darker by the
minute as the sun set completely, and she was
comforted by the shield of night. "Why?" Quinlan
finally asked.

It was easier to talk now, after that little bit of
laughter and with the growing darkness conceal-
ing both their expressions. She felt herself
relaxing, uncurling from her protective knot.

"It was odd," she said, "but I don't think he
wanted me to be sensual. He wanted me to be his
perfect princess, his living, breathing Barbie doll.
I had gotten used to his protectiveness while we

were dating, so at first I didn't think anything of it when he wanted to be with me every time I set foot outside the door. Somehow he always came up with a reason why I shouldn't put in for this job, or that one, and why I couldn't continue working with him. He went shopping with me, picked out my clothes...at first, it all seemed so flattering. My friends were so impressed by the way he treated me.

"Then he began to find reasons why I shouldn't see my friends, why first this one and then that one wasn't 'good' for me. I couldn't invite them over, and he didn't want me visiting them, or meeting them anywhere for lunch. He began vetting my phone calls. It was all so gradual," she said in a faintly bewildered tone. "And he was so gentle. He seemed to have a good reason for everything he did, and he was always focused on me, giving me the kind of attention all women think they want. He only wanted what was best for me, he said."

Quinlan was beginning to feel uneasy. He shifted position, leaning his back against one of the chairs and stretching out in a relaxed position that belied his inner tension. "A control freak," he growled.

"I think we'd been married about six months before I really noticed how completely he'd cut me off from everyone and everything except him," she continued. "I began trying to shift the balance of power, to make a few decisions for myself, if only in minor things, such as where I got my hair cut."

"Let me make another guess. All of a sudden he wasn't so gentle, right?"

"He was furious that I'd gone to a different place. He took the car keys away from me. That was when I really became angry, for the first time. Until then, I'd made excuses, because he'd been so gentle and loving with me. I'd never defied him until then, but when he took the keys out of my purse I lost my temper and yelled at him. He knocked me down," she said briefly.

Quinlan surged to his feet, raw fury running through him so powerfully that he couldn't sit there any longer. To hell with trying to look relaxed. He paced the lobby like a tiger, naked and primitive, the powerful muscles in his body flexing with every movement.

Elizabeth kept on talking. Now that she had started, she wanted to tell it all. Funny, but reliving it wasn't as traumatic as she had expected, not as bad as it had been in her memories and nightmares. Maybe it was having someone else with her that blunted the pain, because always before she had been alone with it.

"I literally became his prisoner. Whenever I tried to assert myself in any way, he'd punish me. There was no pattern to it. Most of the time he would slap me, or even whip me, but sometimes he would just yell, and I never knew what to expect. It was as if he knew that yelling instead of hitting me made it even worse, because then the next time I *knew* he'd hit me, and I'd try, oh, I'd try so hard, not to do anything that would cause the next time. But I always did. I was so nervous that I always did something. Or he'd make up a reason.

"Looking back," she said slowly, "it's hard to believe I was so stupid. By the time I realized what he had done and started trying to fight back, he had me so isolated, so brainwashed, that I literally felt powerless. I had no money, no friends, no car. I was ashamed for anyone to know what was happening. That was what was so sick, that he could convince me it was my fault. I did try to run away once, but he'd paid the doorman to call him if I left, and he found me within half an hour. He didn't hit me that time. He just tied me to the bed and left me. The terror of waiting, helpless, for him to come back and punish me was so bad that hitting me would have been a relief, because that would have meant it was over. Instead he kept me tied for two days, and I nearly became hysterical every time he came into the room."

Quinlan had stopped pacing. He was standing motionless, but she could feel the tension radiating from him.

"He put locks on the phone so I couldn't call out, or even answer it," she said. "But one day he blacked my eye. I don't even remember why. It didn't take much to set him off. When I looked in the mirror the next morning, all of a sudden something clicked in my brain and I knew I had to either get away from him or kill him. I couldn't live like that another day, another hour."

"I'd have opted for killing him," Quinlan said tonelessly. "I may yet."

"After that, it was all so easy," she murmured, ignoring him. "I just packed my suitcases and walked out. The doorman saw me and reached for the phone...and then stopped. He looked at my eye and let the phone drop back into the cradle, and then he opened the door for me and asked if he could call a cab for me. When I told him I didn't have any money, he pulled out his wallet and gave me forty dollars.

"I went to a shelter for abused women. It was the hardest, most humiliating thing I've ever done. It's strange how the women are the ones who are so embarrassed," she said reflectively. "Never the men who have beaten them, terrorized them. *They* seem to think it was their right, or that the women deserved it. But I understand how the women feel, because I was one of them. Its like standing up in public and letting everyone see how utterly stupid you are, what bad judgment you have, what horrible mistakes you've made. The women I met there could barely look anyone in the eye, and they were the victims!

"I got a divorce. It was that simple. With the photographs taken at the shelter, I had evidence of abuse, and Eric would have done anything to preserve his reputation. Oh, he tried to talk me into coming back, he made all sorts of promises, he swore things would be different. I was even tempted," she admitted. "But I couldn't trust my own judgment any longer, so the safest thing, the only thing to do was stay away from romantic relationships in general and Eric Landers in particular."

God, it was so plain now. Quinlan could barely breathe with the realization of the mistakes he'd made in dealing with her. No wonder she had pulled away from him. Because he'd wanted her so much, he had tried to take over, tried to coddle and protect her. It was a normal male instinct, but nothing else could have been more calculated to set off her inner alarms. When she had needed space, he had crowded her, so determined to have her that he hadn't let anything stand in his way. Instead of binding her to him, he had made her run.

"I'm not like Landers," he said hoarsely. "I'll never abuse you, Elizabeth, I swear."

She was silent, and he could sense the sadness

in her. "How can I trust you?" she finally asked. "How can I trust *myself?* What if I make the wrong decision about you, too? You're a much stronger man than Eric could ever hope to be, both physically and mentally. What if you *did* try to hurt me? How could I protect myself? You want to be in charge. You admit it. You're dominating and secretive. God, Quinlan, I love you, but you scare me to death."

His heart surged wildly in his chest at her words. He had known it, but this was the first time she had actually said so. She loved him! At the same time he was suddenly terrified, because he didn't see any way he could convince her to trust him. And that was what it was: a matter of trust. She had lost confidence in her own ability to read character.

He didn't know what to do; for the first time in his life he had no plan of action, no viable option. All he had were his instincts, and he was afraid they were all wrong, at least as far as Elizabeth was concerned. He had certainly bungled it so far. He tried to think what his life would be like without her, if he never again could hold her, and the bleakness of the prospect shook him. Even during these past hellish months, when she had avoided him so totally, even refusing to speak to him on the phone, he hadn't felt this way, because he had still thought he would eventually be able to get her back.

He had to have her. No other woman would do. And he wanted her just as she was: elegant, acerbic, independent, wildly passionate in bed. That, at last, he had done right. She had burned bright and hot in his arms.

He suspected that if he asked for an affair, and only that, she would agree. It was the thought of a legal, binding relationship that had sent her running. She had acted outraged when he had mentioned marriage and kids, getting all huffy because he hadn't included her in the decision-making, but in truth it was that very thing that had so terrified her. Had she sensed he had been about to propose? Finding the file had made her furious, but what had sent her fleeing out the door had been the prospect that he wanted more than just a sexual relationship with her. She could handle being intimate with him; it was the thought of giving him legal rights that gave her nightmares.

He cleared his throat. He felt as if he were walking blindfolded through a mine field, but he couldn't just give up. "I have a reason for not talking about myself," he said hesitantly.

Her reply was an ironic, "I'm sure you do."

He stopped, shrugging helplessly. There was nothing he could tell her that wouldn't sound like an outrageous lie. Okay, that had been a dead end.

"I love you."

The words shook him. He'd admitted the truth of it to himself months ago, not long after meeting her, in fact, but it had been so long since he'd said them aloud that he was startled. Oh, he'd said them during his marriage, at first. It had been so easy, and so expected. Now he realized that the words had been easy because he hadn't meant them. When something really mattered, it was a lot harder to get out.

Elizabeth nodded her head. It had gotten so dark that all he could see was the movement, not her expression. "I believe you do," she replied.

"But you still can't trust me with your life."

"If I needed someone to protect me from true danger, I can't think of anyone I would trust more. But for the other times, the day-to-day normal times that make up a true lifetime, I'm terrified of letting someone close enough to ever have that kind of influence on me again."

Quinlan took another mental sidestep. "We could still see each other," he suggested cautiously. "I know I came on too strong. I'll hold it down. I won't pressure you to make any kind of commitment."

"That wouldn't be fair to you. Marriage is what you want."

"I want *you*," he said bluntly. "With or without the legal trappings. We're great in bed together, and we enjoy each other's company. We have fun together. We can do that without being married, if that's all that's making you shy away from me."

"You want to have an affair?" she asked, needing to pin him down on his exact meaning.

"Hell, no. I want everything. The ring, the kids, all of it. But if an affair is all I can have, I'll take it. What do you say?"

She was silent a long time, thinking it over. At last she sighed and said, "I think I'd be a fool to make any decision right now. These aren't normal circumstances. When the power is back on and our lives are back to normal, then I'll decide."

Quinlan had always had the knack of cutting his losses. He took a step toward her. "But I still have tonight," he said in a low tone. "And I don't intend to waste a minute of it."

Chapter Eight

It was much as it had been that other night, and yet it was much more intense. Quinlan made love to her until she literally screamed with pleasure, and then loved her past her embarrassment. The darkness wrapped around them like a heated cocoon, suspending time and restrictions, allowing anything to be possible. The hours seemed endless, unmarked as they were by any clock or other means that civilized man had developed. The streets outside remained dark and mostly empty; he didn't turn on the radio again, because he didn't want the outside world to intrude, and neither did she.

It was too hot to sleep, despite the high ceiling in the lobby that carried the heat upward. They lay on the cushions and talked, their voices not much more than slow murmurs in the sultry heat. Quinlan's big hands never left her bare body, and Elizabeth suspended her thoughts for this one magic night. She became drowsy, but all inclination to sleep fled when he turned to her in the thick, heated darkness, pressing down on her, his callused hands stroking and probing until she writhed on the cushions. His lovemaking was as steamy as the night, as enveloping. In the darkness she had no inhibitions. She not only let him do as he wanted with her, she reveled in it. There wasn't an inch of her body that he didn't explore.

Daylight brought sunlight and steadily increasing temperatures, but the power remained off. Even though she knew it was impossible to see inside through the glazed windows, she was glad that they could remain snugly hidden in their own little lair. They drank water and ate, and Elizabeth insisted on washing off again in the smothering heat of the rest room, though she knew it wouldn't do any good to clean up with Quinlan waiting impatiently for her outside. Did the man never get tired?

She heard other voices and froze, panicking at the thought of being caught naked in the rest room. Had the power come back on? Impossible, because it was dark in the bathroom. Or had the guard cut off the lights in here before he'd left the day before? She hadn't even thought to check the switch.

Then she heard a familiar call sign and relaxed. The radio, of course. A bit irritated, with herself for being scared and with him because he'd caused it, she strode out of the rest room. "I nearly had a heart attack," she snapped. "I thought someone had come in and I was caught in the rest room."

Quinlan grinned. "What about me? I'm as naked as you are."

He was still sprawled on the cushions, but somehow he looked absolutely at home in his natural state. She looked down at herself and laughed. "I can't believe this is happening."

He stared to say, *It'll be something to tell our grandkids,* but bit the words back. She wouldn't want to hear it, and he'd promised he wouldn't push her. He held out his hand to her, and she crawled onto the cushions with him, sinking into his arms.

"What was on the news?"

"A relatively quiet night in Dallas, though there was some sporadic looting. The same elsewhere. It was just too damn hot to do anything very strenuous."

"Oh, yeah?" she asked, giving him a sidelong glance.

He laughed and deftly rolled her onto her back, mounting her with a total lack of haste that demonstrated how many times during the night he'd done the same thing. "The news?" she prompted.

He nuzzled her neck, breathing in the sweet woman scent. "Oh, that. The national guard has been mobilized from Texas to the East Coast. There were riots in Miami, but they're under control now."

"I thought you said things were relatively quiet?"

"That *is* quiet. With electricity off in almost a quarter of the country, that's amazingly quiet." He didn't want to talk about the blackout. Having Elizabeth naked under him went to his head faster than the most potent whiskey. He kissed her, acutely savoring her instant response, even as he positioned her for his penetration and smoothly slid within. He felt the delicious tightening of her inner muscles as she adjusted to him, the way her fingers dug into his shoulders as she tried to arch even closer to him. His feelings for her swamped him, and he found himself wishing the electricity would never come back on.

Afterward, she yawned and nestled down on his shoulder. "Did the radio announcers say when the power company officials thought the power would be back on?"

"Maybe by this afternoon," he said.

So soon? She felt a bit indignant, as if she had been promised a vacation and now it had been cut short. But this wasn't a vacation; for a lot of people, it was a crisis. Electricity could mean the difference between life and death for someone who was ill. If all they had was a few more hours, she meant to make the best of them.

It seemed that he did, too. Except for insisting that they regularly drink water, he kept her in his arms. Even when he finally tired and had to take a break from lovemaking, he remained nestled within her body. Elizabeth was too tired to think; all she could do was feel. Quinlan had so completely dominated her senses that she would have been alarmed, if she hadn't seen the same drugged expression in his eyes that she knew was in hers. This wasn't something he was doing to her; it was something they were sharing.

They dozed, their sweaty bodies pressed tightly together despite the heat.

It was the wash of cool air over her skin that woke her, shivering.

Quinlan sat up. "The power's back on," he said, squinting up at the overhead lights that seemed to be glaring after the long hours without them. He looked at his watch. "It's eleven o'clock."

"That's too soon," Elizabeth said grumpily. "They said it would be this afternoon."

"They probably gave themselves some extra time in case something went wrong."

Feeling incredibly exposed in the artificial light, Elizabeth scrambled into her clothing. She looked at her discarded panty hose in distaste and crumpled them up, then threw them into the trash.

"What do we do now?" she asked, pushing her hair back.

Quinlan zipped his pants. "Now we go home."

"How? Do we call the guard service?"

"Oh, I'll call them all right. Later. I have a few things to say. But now that the power's on, I can get us out of here."

While he tapped into the security system, Elizabeth hastily straightened the furniture, shoving it back into place and restoring all the cushions to their original sites. A blush was already heating her face at the possibility of anyone finding out about their love nest, literally in the middle of the lobby. She didn't know if she would ever be able to walk into this building again without blushing.

Quinlan grunted with satisfaction as he entered a manual override into the system that would allow him to open the side door. "Come on," he said, grabbing Elizabeth's hand.

She barely had time to snatch up her purse before he was hustling her out of there. She blinked in the blinding sunshine. The heat rising off the sidewalk was punishing. "We can't just leave the building unlocked," she protested.

"I didn't. It locked again as soon as the door

closed." Taking her arm, he steered her around the corner and across the street to the parking deck.

Before she could react, he was practically stuffing her into his car. "I have my own car!" she said indignantly.

"I know. Don't worry, it isn't going anywhere. But we don't know that the electricity is on all over the city, and we don't know what kind of situation you'll find at your place. Until I know you're safe, I'm keeping you with me."

It was the sort of high-handed action that had always made her uneasy in the past, but now it didn't bother her. Maybe it was because she was so sleepy. Maybe it was because he was right. For whatever reason, she relaxed in the seat and let her eyes close.

He had to detour a couple of times to reach her apartment, but the traffic was surprisingly light, and it didn't take long, not even as long as normal. She didn't protest when he went inside with her. The electricity was on there, too, the central air conditioning humming as it tried to overcome the built-up heat.

"Into the shower," Quinlan commanded.

She blinked at him. "What?"

He put his arm around her, turning her toward her bedroom. "The shower. We're both going to take a nice, cool shower. We're in good shape, but this will make us feel better. Believe me, we're a little dehydrated."

Their bargain had been only for the night, but since it had already extended into the day, she supposed it wouldn't hurt to carry it a little further. She allowed him to strip her and wasn't at all surprised when he undressed and climbed in with her. The shower spray was cool enough to raise a chill, and it felt wonderful. She turned around to let it wash over her spine and tilted her head back so the water soaked through her sweat-matted hair.

"Feel good?" he murmured, running his hands over her. She would have thought that he was washing her, except that he wasn't using soap.

"Mmm." He bent his head and Elizabeth lifted hers. If only she could stay this way, she thought. Kissing him, being kissed by him. His hard arms locked around her. Feeling him so close, all worries pushed aside...

The cool shower was revitalizing in more ways than one. Abruptly he lifted her and braced her against the wall, and she gasped as he drove deep into her. There was nothing slow about it this time; he took her fiercely, as wild as he had been the day before on the floor of the lobby, as if all those times in between had never been.

Later they went to bed. She could barely hold her eyes open while he dried her hair, then carried her to the bed and placed her between the cool, smooth sheets. She sighed, every muscle relaxing, and immediately went to sleep, not knowing that he slipped into bed beside her.

Still, she wasn't surprised when she woke during the afternoon and he was there. Lazily she let her gaze drift over his strong-boned features. He needed to shave; the black beard lay on his skin like a dark shadow. His hair was tousled, and his closed eyelids looked as delicate as a child's. Odd, for she had never thought of Quinlan as delicate in any way, never associated any sort of softness with him. Yet he had been tender with her, even in his passion. It wasn't the same type of gentleness Eric had displayed; Eric had been gentle, she realized now, because he hadn't *wanted* any responding passion from her. He had wanted her to be nothing more than a doll, to be dressed and positioned and shown off for his own ego. Quinlan, on the other hand, had been as helpless in his passion as she had been in hers.

Her body quivered at his nearness. Still half asleep, she pushed at him. His eyes opened immediately, and he rolled onto his back. "What's wrong?"

"Plenty," she said, slithering on top of him and feeling the immediate response between his legs. "It's been at least—" She paused to look at the clock, but it was blinking stupidly at her, not having been reset since the power had come back on. "It's been too damn long since I've had this." She reached between his legs, and he sucked in his breath, his back arching as she guided him into place.

"God, I'm sorry," he apologized fervently, and bit back a moan as she moved on him. This was the way he had always known his Elizabeth could be, hot with uncomplicated passion, a little bawdy, intriguingly earthy. She made him dizzy with delight.

Her eyes were sultry, her lips swollen and pouty from his kisses, her dark hair tumbling over her shoulders. He watched her expression tighten with desire as she moved slowly up and down on him, her eyes closing even more. "Just for that," she murmured, "I get to be on top."

He reached overhead and caught the headboard, his powerful biceps flexing as his fists locked around the brass bars. "No matter how I beg and plead?"

"No matter what you say," she assured him, and gasped herself as her movements wrenched another spasm of pleasure from her nerve endings.

"Good." Quinlan arched, almost lifting her off the bed. "Then I won't accidentally say something that will make you quit."

He didn't. When she collapsed, exhausted, on his chest, they were both numb with pleasure. He thrust his hand into her tangled hair and held her almost desperately close. She inhaled the hot, musky scent of his skin, and with the slightest of motions rubbed her cheek against the curly hair on his chest. She could feel his heart thudding under her ear, and the strong rhythm was reassuring. They slept again, and woke in the afternoon with the sun going down in a blaze of red and gold, to drowsily make love again.

He got up to turn on the television sitting on her dresser, then returned to bed to hold her while they watched the news, which was, predictably, all about the blackout. Elizabeth felt a little bemused, as if a national crisis had passed without her knowing about it, even though she had been intimately embroiled in this one. Intimately, she thought, in more ways than one. Perhaps that was why she felt so out of touch with reality. She hadn't spent the past twenty-four hours concentrating on the lack of electricity, she had been concentrating on Quinlan.

The Great Blackout, as the Dallas newscasters were calling it, had disrupted electrical services all over the Sun Belt. The heat wave, peak usage and solar flares had all combined to overload and blow circuits, wiping out entire power grids. Elizabeth felt as if her own circuits had been seriously damaged by Quinlan's high-voltage lovemaking.

He spent the night with her. He didn't ask if he could, and she didn't tell him that he couldn't.

She knew that she was only postponing the inevitable, but she wanted this time with him.
Telling him about Eric hadn't changed her mind,
any more than knowing about Eric had changed
Quinlan's basic character.

When morning came, they both knew that the
time-out had ended. Reality couldn't be held at
bay any longer.

"So what happens now?" he asked quietly.

She looked out the window as she sipped her
coffee. It was Saturday; neither of them had to
work, though Quinlan had already talked to a
couple of his staffers, placing the calls almost as
soon as he'd gotten out of bed. She knew that all
she had to say was one word, "Stay," and they
would spend the weekend in bed, too. It would be
wonderful, but come Monday, it would make it
just that much more difficult to handle.

"I don't see that the situation has changed," she
finally said.

"Damn it, Elizabeth!" He got up, his big body
coiled with tension. "Can you honestly say that
I'm anything like Landers?"

"You're very dominating," she pointed out.

"You love me."

"At the time, I thought I loved him, too. What if
I'm wrong again?" Her eyes were huge and stark
as she stared at him. "There's no way you can

know how bad it was without having lived through it yourself. I would rather die than go through anything like that again. I don't know how I can afford to take the chance on you. I still don't know *you,* not the way you know me. You're so secretive that I can't tell who you really are. How can I trust you when I don't know you?"

"And if you did?" he asked in a harsh tone. "If you knew all there is to know about me?"

"I don't know," she said; then they looked at each other and broke into snickering laughter. "There's a lot of knowing and not knowing in a few short sentences."

"At least we know what we mean," he said, and she groaned; then they started laughing again. When he sobered, he reached out and slid his hand underneath her heavy curtain of hair, clasping the back of her neck. "Let me give something a try," he urged. "Let me have another shot at changing your mind."

"Does this mean that if it doesn't work, you'll stop trying?" she asked wryly, and had to laugh at the expression on his face. "Oh, Tom, you don't even have a clue about how to give up, do you?"

He shrugged. "I've never wanted anyone the way I want you," he said, smiling back just as wryly. "But at least I've made some progress. You've started calling me Tom again."

He dressed and roughly kissed her as he started out the door. "I'll be back as soon as I can. It may not be today. But there's something I want to show you before you make a final decision."

Elizabeth leaned against the door after she had closed it behind him. Final decision? She didn't know whether to laugh or cry. To her, the decision had been final for the past six months. So why did she feel that, unless she gave him the answer he wanted, she would still be explaining her reasons to him five years from now?

Chapter Nine

The doorbell rang just before five on Sunday morning. Elizabeth stumbled groggily out of bed, staring at the clock in bewilderment. She had finally set the thing, but surely she had gotten it wrong. Who would be leaning on her doorbell at 4:54 in the morning?

"Quinlan," she muttered, moving unsteadily down the hall.

She looked through the peephole to make certain, though she really hadn't doubted it. Yawning, she released the chain and locks and opened the door. "Couldn't it have waited another few hours?" she asked grouchily, heading toward the kitchen to put on a pot of coffee. If she had to deal with him at this hour, she needed to be more alert than she was right now.

"No," he said. "I haven't slept, and I want to get this over with."

She hadn't slept all that much herself; after he'd left the morning before, she had wandered around the apartment, feeling restless and unable to settle on anything to do. It had taken her a while to identify it, but at last she had realized that she was lonely. He had been with her for thirty-six hours straight, holding her while they slept, making love, talking, arguing, laughing. The blackout had forced them into a hothouse intimacy, leading her to explore old nightmares and maybe even come to terms with them.

The bed had seemed too big, too cold, too empty. For the first time she began to question whether or not she had been right in breaking off with him. Quinlan definitely was *not* Eric Landers. Physically, she felt infinitely safe and cherished with him; on that level, at least, she didn't think he would ever hurt her.

It was the other facet of his personality that worried her the most, his secrecy and insistence on being in control. She had some sympathy with the control thing; after all, she was a bit fanatic on the subject herself. The problem was that she had had to fight so hard to get herself back, how could she risk her identity again? Quinlan was as relentless as the tides; lesser personalities crumbled before him. She didn't know anything about huge chunks of his life, what had made him the man he was. What if he were hiding something from her that she absolutely couldn't live with? What if there was a darkness to his soul that he could keep under control until it was too late for her to protect herself?

She was under no illusions about marriage. Even in this day and age, it gave a man a certain autonomy over his wife. People weren't inclined to get involved in domestic "disputes," even when the dispute involved a man beating the hell out of his smaller, weaker wife. Some police departments were starting to view it more seriously, but they were so inundated with street crime, drug and highway carnage that, objectively, she could see how a woman's swollen face or broken arm didn't seem as critical when weighed in that balance.

And marriage was what Quinlan wanted. If she resumed a relationship with him, he might not mention it for a while—she gave him a week, at the outside—but he would be as relentless in his pursuit of that goal as he was in everything else. She loved him so much that she knew he would eventually wear her down, which was why she had to make a final decision now. And she *could* do it now—if the answer was no. She still had enough strength to walk away from him, in her own best interests. If she waited, every day would weaken that resolve a little more.

He had been silent while she moved around the kitchen, preparing the coffeemaker and turning it on. Hisses and gurgles filled the air as the water heated; then came the soft tinkle of water into the pot and the delicious aroma of fresh coffee filled the room.

"Let's sit down," he said, and placed his briefcase on the table. It was the first time she had noticed it.

She shook her head. "If this requires thinking, at least wait until I've had a cup of coffee."

His mouth quirked. "I don't know. Somehow I think I'd stand a better chance if your brain stayed in neutral and you just went with your instincts."

"Hormones, you mean."

"I have nothing against those, either." He rubbed his beard and sighed wearily. "But I guess I could use a cup of coffee, too."

He had taken the time to change clothes, she saw; he was wearing jeans that looked to be at least ten years old, and a soft, white, cotton shirt. But his eyes were circled with dark rings and were bloodshot from lack of sleep, and he obviously hadn't shaved since the morning before the blackout. The blackness of his heavy beard made him look like a ruffian; actually, he looked exactly like the type of people he hired.

When the coffee stopped dripping, she filled two mugs and slid one in front of him as she took a seat at the table. Cautiously sipping the hot brew, she wondered how long it would take to hit the bloodstream.

He opened the briefcase and took out two files, one very thin and the other over an inch thick. He slid the thin one toward her. "Okay, read this one first."

She opened it and lifted her eyebrows when she saw that it was basically the same type of file that he'd had on her, though this one was on himself. Only it seemed to be rather sketchy. *Bare bones* was more like it, and even then, part of the skeleton was missing. It gave his name, birthdate, birthplace, social security number, physical description, education and present employment, as well as the sketchy facts of his brief marriage, so many years ago. Other than that, he seemed not to have existed between the years of his divorce and when he had started his security business.

"Were you in cold storage for about fifteen years?" she finally asked, shoving the file back toward him. "I appreciate the gesture, but if this was supposed to tell me about you, it lacks a little something."

He eyed her warily, then grinned. "Not many people can manage to be sarcastic at five o'clock in the morning."

"At five o'clock, that's about all I *can* manage."

"I'll remember that," he murmured, and slid the second file, the thick one, toward her. "This is the information you wouldn't have gotten if you investigated me."

Her interest level immediately soared, and she flipped the manila folder open. The documents before her weren't originals, but were a mixture of photostats and faxes. She looked at the top of one and then gave him a startled look. "Government, huh?"

"I had to get a buddy to pull up my file and send it to me. Nothing in there is going to reveal state secrets, but the information is protected, for my sake. I could have hacked into the computer, but I'd just as soon not face a jail term, so it took some time to get it all put together."

"Just exactly what did you do?" she asked, not at all certain that she wanted to know. After being so frustrated by his lack of openness, now that his life lay open before her, she wasn't all that eager to know the details. If he had been shot at, if he had been in danger in any way…that could give her a different set of nightmares.

"No Hollywood stuff," he assured her, grinning.

"I'm disappointed. You mean you weren't a secret agent?" Relieved was more like it.

"That's a Hollywood term. In the business, it's

called a field operative. And no, that isn't what I did. I gathered information, set up surveillance and security systems, worked with antiterrorist squads. It wasn't the kind of job that you talk over with your buddies in the bar after work."

"I can understand that. You got in the habit of not talking about yourself or what you did."

"It was more than just a habit, it could have meant people's lives. I still don't talk about it, because I still know people in the business. Information is the greatest asset a government can have, and the most dangerous."

She tapped the file. "So why are you showing me this?"

"Because I trust you," he said simply; then another grin spread across his face. "And because I didn't think you'd believe me if I just said, 'I can't talk about myself, government stuff, very hush-hush.' You would have laughed in my face. It's the kind of crap you hear in singles bars, hot-shot studs trying to impress the airheads. You aren't an airhead."

After flipping a few pages and scanning them, she said, "You're right. I wouldn't have believed this. Most people don't do this type of work."

He shrugged. "Like I said, I went to Cal Tech, and I was very good at what I did."

"Did?" she asked incredulously. "It's what you still do. It's just that now you do it for yourself instead of the government." An idea struck her. "The people you hire. Are they—?"

"Some of them," he admitted.

"Like the biker?"

He laughed. "Like the biker. Hell, do you think I'd hire anyone who looked like that if I didn't personally know him? He really was an operative, one mean son of a bitch."

"They come to you for jobs when they retire?"

"No, nothing like that. I'm not a halfway house for burned-out government employees. I keep track of people, contact them to see if they're interested in working for me. Most of them are very normal, and it's just a matter of moving from one computer job to another."

She closed the file and pushed it away from her. Quinlan eyed her with alarm. "Aren't you going to read it?"

"No. I don't need to know every detail of everything you've done. A brief overview is enough."

He drew a deep breath and sat back. "Okay. That's it, then. I've done all I can. I can't convince you, prove it to you in any way, that I'll never treat you the way Landers did. *I* know I won't, but you're the one who has to believe it. Elizabeth, sweetheart, will you marry me?"

She couldn't help it. She knew it wasn't the way a woman was supposed to respond to a marriage proposal, but the relentlessness of it was so typical of Tom Quinlan that she couldn't stop the sharp crack of laughter from exploding into sound. She would probably hear that question every day until she either gave him the answer he wanted or went mad under the pressure. Instead of making her feel pressured, as it would have before, there was a certain amount of comfort in knowing she could depend on him to that extent. Seeing that file had meant more to her than he could know. It wasn't just that it filled in the gaps of his life, but that he trusted her to know about him.

She managed to regain her composure and stared seriously at him. Somehow, what had happened during the blackout had lessened the grip that Eric Landers had still had on her, even after so many years. During the long hours of that hot night she had been forced to truly look at what had happened, to deal with it, and for the first time she'd realized that Eric had still held her captive. Because of him, she had been afraid to truly let herself live. She was still afraid, but all of a sudden she was more afraid of losing what she had. If it were possible to lose Quinlan, she thought, looking at him with wry fondness. But, yes, she could lose him, if she didn't start appreciating the value of what he was offering her. It was sink or swim time.

He had begun to fidget under her silent regard.

She inhaled deeply. "Marriage, huh? No living together, seeing how it works?"

"Nope. Marriage. The love and honor vows. Until death."

She scowled a little at him. He was as yielding as rock when he made up his mind about something. "Yours could come sooner than you think," she muttered.

"That's okay, if you're the one who does me in. I have an idea of the method you'd use," he replied, and a look of startlingly intense carnal hunger crossed his face. He shivered a little, then gathered himself and raised his right hand. "I swear I'll be an absolute pussycat of a husband. A woman like you needs room."

She had taken a sip of coffee, and at his words she swallowed wrong, choking on the liquid. She coughed and wheezed, then stared at him incredulously. "Then why haven't you been giving me any?" she yelled.

"Because I was afraid to give you enough room to push me away," he said. He gave her a little half smile that acknowledged his own vulnerability and held out his hand to her. "You scare me, too, babe. I'm scared to death you'll decide you can get along without me."

She crossed her arms and glared at him, refusing to take his outstretched hand. "If you think you'll get a little slave, you'll be disappointed. I won't pick up after you, I don't like cooking and I won't tolerate dirty clothes strewn all over the place."

A grin began to spread across his face as she talked, a look of almost blinding elation, but he only said mildly, "I'm fairly neat, for a man."

"Not good enough. I heard that qualification."

He sighed. "All right. We'll write it into our wedding vows. I'll keep my clothes picked up, wash the whiskers out of the sink and put the lid back down on the toilet. I'll get up with the kids—"

"Kids?" she asked delicately.

He lifted his brows at her. She stifled a smile. God, dealing with him was exhilarating! "Okay," she said, relenting. "Kids. But not more than two."

"Two sounds about right. Deal?"

She pretended to consider, then said, "Deal," and they solemnly shook hands.

Quinlan sighed with satisfaction, then hauled her into his arms, literally dragging her across the table and knocking her mug of coffee to the floor. Oblivious to the spreading brown puddle, he held her on his lap and kissed her until her knees were weak. When he lifted his head, a big grin creased his face and he said, "By the way, I always know how to bypass my own systems."

She put her hand on his rough jaw and kissed him again. "I know," she said smugly.

* * *

Over an hour later, he lifted his head from the pillow and scowled at her. "There's no way you could have known."

"Not for certain, but I suspected." She stretched, feeling lazy and replete. Her entire body throbbed with a pleasant, lingering heat.

He gathered her close and pressed a kiss to the top of her head. "Six months," he grumbled. "And it took a damn blackout to get you to talk to me."

"I feel rather fond of the blackout," she murmured. "Without it, I wouldn't have been forced to spend so much time with you."

"Are you saying we never would have worked it out if it hadn't been for that?"

"I wouldn't have given you the chance to get that close to me," she said, her voice quiet with sincerity. "I wasn't playing games, Tom. I was scared to death of you, and of losing myself again. You never would have had the chance to convince me, if it hadn't been for the blackout."

"Then God bless overloaded power grids," he muttered. "But I'd have gotten to you, one way or another."

"Other than kidnapping, I can't think how," she replied caustically.

He went very still, and the silence made her lift her head to give him a suspicious glare. He tried to look innocent, then gave it up when he saw she wasn't buying it.

"That was what I had planned for the weekend, if you refused to have dinner with me Thursday night," he admitted a bit sheepishly.

"Ah-ha. I *thought* you waylaid me that afternoon."

"A man has to do something when his woman won't give him the time of day," he muttered. "I was desperate."

She said, "It's six-thirty."

A brief flicker of confusion crossed his face; then he glanced at the clock and grinned. "So it is," he said with satisfaction. She had just given him the time of day—and a lot more. With a lithe twist of his powerful body he tumbled her back into the twisted sheets and came down on top of her.

"I love you," he rumbled. "And I still haven't heard the 'yes' I've been waiting for."

"I agreed. We made a deal."

"I know, but I'm a little more traditional than that. Elizabeth Major, will you marry me?"

She hesitated for a second. Eric Landers had lost the power to keep her a victim. "Yes, Tom Quinlan, I certainly will."

He lowered his head to kiss her. When he surfaced, they were both breathing hard and knew it would be a while yet before they got out of bed. He gave the clock another glance. "Around nine," he murmured, "remind me to make a couple of phone calls. I need to cancel the kidnapping plans."

She laughed, and kept laughing until his strong thrust into her body changed the laughter into a soft cry of pleasure, as he turned that relentless focus to the task of bringing them both to the intense ecstasy they found only with each other. She had been so afraid of that part of him, but now she knew it was what made him a man she could depend on for the rest of her life. As she clung to his shoulders, a dim echo of thought floated through her brain: "God bless overloads!"

Also by Linda Howard

A GAME OF CHANCE
ISBN 978-0-7278-8968-3

Searching for a mysterious and elusive terrorist, undercover agent
Chance Mackenzie sets out to use the man's daughter, Sunny Miller, as
bait to discover her father's location – only to learn that the innocent
beauty is running for her own life.

LOVING EVANGELINE
ISBN 978-0-7278-8901-0

Evangeline Shaw is the key to the conspiracy that threatens Robert Can-
non's company. Robert tracks her to a small town in Alabama, but as he
tries to untangle the knot that surrounds her, he finds himself questioning
everything he believed. Are Robert's feelings clouding his judgment
when it comes to the woman who has to be guilty as sin?

THE COURTSHIP OF CAROL SOMMARS
ISBN 978-0-7278-9063-4

Peter Sommars is fifteen and wants a little more independence, which is why he'd like his mom, Carol, to start dating. He even knows the perfect man – Alex Preston, his best friend's dad. As it turns out, Alex is interested, but Carol's doing everything she can to sidestep his pursuit, which only makes him – and the boys – more determined.

THE BEST MISTAKE
ISBN 978-0-7278-8927-0

Zoe Fleming is a hardworking single mom – and she loves it, though she would like a tenant to share household expenses. What she gets is confirmed bachelor Coop, who quickly befriends her son and in no time has the reluctant Zoe charmed, too. Could this be a recipe for disaster, or the best mistake she's ever made?